Camel Caravan

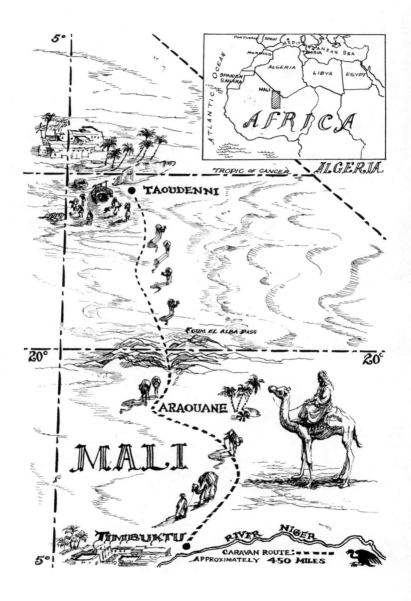

5°

PORTUGAL SPAIN
MEDITERRANEAN SEA
MOROCCO TUNISIA
SPANISH SAHARA
ALGERIA LIBYA EGYPT
MALI
ATLANTIC OCEAN

AFRICA

ALGERIA

TROPIC OF CANCER

● TAOUDENNI

FOUM EL ALBA PASS

20°   20°

ARAOUANE

MALI

TIMBUKTU   RIVER   NIGER

5°   CARAVAN ROUTE: ▄ ▄ ▄
APPROXIMATELY 450 MILES

Weekly Reader Children's Book Club presents

Camel Caravan

BY ARTHUR CATHERALL

Drawings by Joseph Papin

THE SEABURY PRESS
New York

Contents

ONE

The Baby Camel

"This could not have happened at a worse time."

Moussa, the camel man, was frowning as he stared at the beautiful little creature squatting in the sand. The young camel was no more than ten minutes old, and its mother was licking it carefully from head to foot.

"Why do our father and our Uncle Abbah frown so?" Fedada asked her older brother. "Surely any time a baby camel is born is a time for gladness."

Twelve-year-old Youba snorted. "Only a girl would say a thing like that. Do we not start tomorrow with the salt caravan for Timbuktu?"

The boy turned to gaze at the nearby salt pits. Around each deep hole half-naked men were working; some poured water into the pits while others dug at the wet salt. Loaded into buckets the salt was then hauled to the surface by workers whose bodies shone with sweat. Other men were filling six-inch-deep wooden boxes with the wet salt, then ramming it hard. In a day the sun would dry out every drop of moisture, leaving a block of hard, solid salt in each box. When the blocks were completely dry they would be shaken out and stacked, ready to be loaded onto camels.

Had there not been salt below the surface of the desert, the village of Taoudenni, a mile away, would never have existed. Youba could see its houses, shimmering white in the pitiless glare of the sun.

Salt in Taoudenni cost no more than $1.50 a block, but after it had been carried across the desert to the traders at Timbuktu, its price would be $15 a block. In the great heat of west Africa, neither man nor beast could live without salt, and traders in Timbuktu awaited with eagerness the twice yearly salt caravans from the north, made up of camel men like Youba's father and uncle.

It was Uncle Abbah who broke the silence and brought Youba's attention back to the newborn camel. "One good thing, my brother," he said to Youba's father. "This baby looks as if he could grow up to be a king of camels. He reminds me of the *mehari* you once owned—what was he called?"

"Ah, Amr'r," Moussa murmured, his dark eyes lighting up for a moment. Youba and Fedada remembered Amr'r too. They had never seen the famous milk-white racing camel, but they had heard countless tales of his wonderful strength and speed.

"Let us call this one Amr'r, Father," Fedada pleaded. "He is so lovely. Look at his slender legs."

"It is his legs which worry me," her father said soberly. "His mother is one of my best camels, and she will walk the desert well enough even though she has to feed him. But her son can never keep pace with the rest of the caravan."

"And there is the question of feeding," Uncle Abbah pointed out to the children. "A camel so young must be fed every two or three hours. That means a halt, and you know the caravan stops only at noon, the end of the day, or when we reach a water hole."

The roaring protest of a camel being made to rise distracted the little family group. All around the salt pits groups of camels were standing or sitting down. Camel owners and their servants were busy with last-minute preparations, for the big caravan would be starting south early the next morning. Ropes and saddles were being tested and repaired. The all-important *gerbas* — goatskin water bags — were being checked for leaks.

Youba gazed with wonder at the young camel. "Amr'r *would* be a good name for him." He touched his father's sleeve. "Do you not remember, my father? You promised that when I was old enough to work with you, the first baby camel to be born would be mine."

Without waiting for a reply, the boy bent down to stroke the baby camel's head, but Tamerouelt, the mother, suddenly shot out her long neck. She snapped at Youba and at the same time a snarling, gurgling roar came from her throat.

Youba drew back in alarm, and his Uncle Abbah chuckled as he said, "That is one thing you must learn, my nephew. Never try to stroke a newborn camel — if the mother is near."

Youba nodded; then, as his father still said nothing, he renewed his plea: "Please say that we can take Amr'r with us, my father."

"I am trying to think what we can do," Moussa said. "If the camel had been born a week ago I might have taken a chance. But you know the way is hard, Youba. Your sister is eleven years old, and she did not find it easy even though she rode many miles of the trip. A baby camel cannot ride."

"Did I ever complain?" asked Fedada.

"No, no — I didn't mean that," her father said quickly. "You behaved very well the entire journey. But I know it was especially hard for you, coming so soon after your mother's death." He rubbed a hand gently across Fedada's dark, shining hair. "I would never have brought you along if there had been any relative you could have stayed with in Timbuktu. You have been very brave, my daughter."

No one spoke for a moment, but the air was filled with sounds: the clanking of windlasses used to haul the salt from the deep holes, and the thump-thump-thump of the flat wooden utensils with which men were beating damp salt into the boxes.

"My brother, I have just had a thought," Uncle

Abbah said, leading Moussa off a little way from the children and the camels. "Tomorrow eight hundred camels start south, but there will be another two hundred left behind — awaiting salt. They will not be able to start for at least another week. Suppose —"

Moussa shook his head. "We cannot wait for the second caravan. Am I a rich man that I can afford to feed forty camels for a week while we wait for a baby camel to get strength in its legs?"

Abbah shrugged, was silent for a few moments, then made another suggestion: "Suppose I stayed behind. You and your man could take thirty camels. Leave ten for me. With my servant and the help of the children, I could handle them. This young camel might then be strong enough —"

Again he stopped, for his elder brother Moussa was shaking his head once more. "I would be worrying about Youba and Fedada," he muttered. "What if the raiders should attack?"

Uncle Abbah frowned. Twice each year the salt caravans left Taoudenni, and twice a year bands of raiders left the Spanish Sahara far to the north. These men of Moorish blood rode magnificent meharis. They were well armed, fierce, and lawless. After riding hundreds of miles they swept onto the caravan routes.

Even when the French had ruled the desert and their famous Camel Corps patrolled the region, the raiders looted caravans. The desert was so vast, and the Moors seemed able to live on no more than a handful of dates and a mouthful of water. They would sweep in at dawn, plunder the merchants, then vanish.

Now that the area was part of the country of Mali the salt merchants had to pay men to act as guards. Caravans were smaller, so they could move more quickly; yet the raiders still seemed to know just when to descend on the caravan routes.

"There is always danger of raiders," Abbah said at last. "But maybe there will be less worry about the children if they do come with the smaller caravan. You know what men are whispering around the fires at night."

Moussa's eyes narrowed, and he looked even more unhappy. How the story had started no one knew; but everyone was saying that a wealthy merchant, disguised as a poor traveler, would be in the big caravan. It was making the camel men uneasy, for it was also whispered that the raiders from the Spanish Sahara had spies in Taoudenni. If this was so, and if they had sent word that a very rich man was with the caravan, there was every likelihood of a dawn attack somewhere in the desert.

"There is less chance of a poorer caravan of only two hundred camels being attacked," Abbah argued. "Perhaps it will be safer for Youba and Fedada to wait here for a week."

"I must have time to think about it," Moussa said. Turning back to Youba, he told his son to keep an eye on Tamerouelt and the baby camel. Then he and his brother walked away together.

Youba and Fedada watched their father and uncle approach a well where a score of camels were drinking from a trough into which men were pouring bucket after bucket of water.

"Do you think our father will sell the baby?" Fedada asked.

"No!" Youba said quickly. "Our father knows a good camel, and this one *is* good, and he is to be mine. He will never be sold!" But Youba's voice did not sound as confident as his words.

After a few minutes, Fedada moved toward their tent. There was millet to be pounded and mixed with dried goat cheese—enough food to last them for six weeks. She left Youba standing guard over the baby camel and its mother.

TWO

Amr'r in Training

Fedada was still pounding millet an hour later when Youba rushed up to the tent. "My sister, I was right! Our father has just told me that he will *not* sell the little camel! Our Uncle Abbah will stay behind with ten camels, and we stay too. We have a week to teach Amr'r how to walk the desert."

"It will not be easy," Fedada murmured. She was remembering how tired she had been on the long journey north from Timbuktu to Taoudenni.

"I am not afraid for him," Youba said confidently. "His mother was a racing camel, and so was his father. You know what they say of mehari camels. They never give up. They die rather than give up."

Fedada nodded. There was a great difference between the ordinary working camel and the proud mehari. The working camel which spends its life carrying heavy and often awkward loads across the desert is a snarling bad-tempered grumbler. It will

bite and spit, and must be led all the time or it flops to its knees. Amr'r, with mehari blood in his veins, could be depended on to walk without a murmur of complaint until his long thin legs crumpled under him.

Next morning, as the sun was rising above the horizon, the caravan of eight hundred heavily laden camels began to move off. There had been bustle and confusion for more than an hour, and the air had been filled with the protesting snarls of camels, the yells of angry men struggling to secure the creatures' burdens, and the bellows of the guards who wanted to get the caravan moving before the

real, blistering heat of the day set in. Laborers who would soon be hauling wet salt from the holes stood and watched in silence.

Youba, Fedada, and their Uncle Abbah helped Moussa and his single servant get their thirty camels loaded and linked nose to tail. Then the man in charge of the guards fired a shot in the air. At once the commotion increased as men called their camels to rise. Hind legs straightened and loads jerked forward, almost threatening to topple over each camel's long neck. Then the animals' slender forelegs straightened out, and within a few minutes all eight hundred camels were moving. They were roped in strings of from a dozen to twenty, and they would keep on moving as long as a man pulled — no matter how lightly — on the rope of the leading camel.

Youba, Fedada, and Uncle Abbah watched Moussa's thirty camels rise. Each sixth camel was laden with food and gerbas full of water. The others carried the precious salt.

There was a worried expression on Moussa's face. Abbah sensed what was passing through his brother's mind and gripped his shoulder, saying, "I will guard Youba and Fedada with my life. Do I not love them as much as you do? One week after you reach Timbuktu, we shall rejoin you. I promise that."

Moussa laid a hand on Youba's arm and held Fedada close with the other. Forcing a smile he said, "Do everything your Uncle Abbah says and all will be well." Then he turned and began to hurry after the camels. They were in their stride now, and the last one was already a good twenty yards ahead of its owner.

Youba and Fedada stood staring after him. Youba felt a strange, tight sensation in his throat and Fedada's eyes were glistening. They had watched their father go off with the camels many times, for in addition to the caravan trips to Taoudenni, Moussa carried goods into the south Niger country.

But then they had been at home in Timbuktu; now in Taoudenni they felt alone and a little afraid, even though their uncle was with them.

Abbah took their minds off their worries by saying, "What about Amr'r? We have only a week to get him strong enough for the desert, so no time must be lost."

The three of them left the caravan track and walked over to Tamerouelt and her baby. Little Amr'r already looked sturdier, and when Youba tickled him, one thin hind leg shot out in a swift kick which brought a grunt of pain from the boy.

"You see, he is already growing up," Fedada chuckled, "and not to be tickled as a baby is tickled."

Abbah told them that all they should do that day was lead Tamerouelt a few yards away from the encampment, and back again. Amr'r would follow her, and they could keep doing this every ten minutes or so. It would get the little camel used to being on his feet.

The real training began early next morning. With Abbah to make sure they did not tire the young camel, Youba and Fedada led Tamerouelt away from the bustle of the salt pits, and Amr'r followed. They went out about a mile into the desert, allowed Amr'r to feed, then walked back. They did that twice more in the afternoon, the last time going almost a mile and a half before halting.

On the third day Tamerouelt refused to walk. She knew that little Amr'r was too stiff from his exertions of the day before, and no matter what Youba and his uncle did, the cream-colored mehari refused to move.

On the fourth day, though, Tamerouelt allowed herself to be led into the desert, and that day and the next the walks grew longer and longer. Fedada stayed back at the camp, for someone had to help the servant watch the ten other camels and their loads of salt, as well as prepare the food and the goatskins for the trek south.

On the sixth morning, when they were moving away from the tent, Youba voiced the uneasiness that had been growing in him during the past two days. "My uncle," he said, "do you really think my camel *can* walk to Timbuktu? He is very young. I know he is brave, but can he keep up with the older camels?"

Abbah tugged at his short dark beard for a moment or so. He was also worried. The tough, grumbling work camels could walk twenty miles in a day, whether it was through soft dune sands or over the hard, stone-littered route through the hills.

"You do not answer me, Uncle," Youba said. "Is it that you think he cannot make the journey?"

"Only Allah has that answer," Abbah said soberly. "We have done all we can. We have fed Amr'r's mother well and given her much water, so her milk should be rich. Her son has grown, and he is much stronger now than when he was born."

"But you don't think he is strong enough," Youba persisted.

"We must do our best to help him," his uncle said. "Tomorrow, take Tamerouelt and Amr'r to the front of the caravan. In that way, when he wishes to stop to nurse, you will not be left behind. I will be near the end, so I shall be close by if the young camel grows too weary."

Seeing that Youba was still not satisfied, Abbah clapped a hand on his shoulder and added, "Tomorrow night, at the end of the first day's march, we should know the answer. Allah is great and merciful. Perhaps he will listen to our prayers and give Amr'r the necessary strength."

Youba and Fedada were both very anxious when the two-hundred-strong caravan gathered on the morning of the seventh day. Like his sister, Youba was dressed in a garment which looked almost like a nightshirt. It was made of cotton, dyed blue-black, and had short wide sleeves, and a hood which could be pulled over the head at night when the blazing heat of the desert was gone. The air was bitterly cold now, and both brother and sister had drawn their hoods up.

Men hurried from camel to camel, making sure the slabs of salt were firmly lashed in place. If a slab fell off, it usually broke into a hundred pieces and had to be left behind. No one wanted that — the salt was too valuable.

Little Amr'r and his mother were at the front of the caravan, as Uncle Abbah had suggested. Now that it was time to start, Youba and Fedada were

wondering if Amr'r would be able to keep up the pace — for the caravan traveled at about two miles an hour, and sometimes a little faster if the sand was firm and flat.

The guards on their magnificent camels trotted along the length of the camel caravan. They shouted at men still knotting salt in place, and finally two went to the head of the caravan. One guard then fired his rifle into the air as a signal to move off.

The camel men shouted, some of them whacking their beasts across the back of the head, and at once the air was filled with a chorus of snarls and that peculiar gargling protest which working camels make when they know that another day's march is beginning.

As if waiting for this moment, the horizon to the east showed a thin line of rich gold. The sun was rising. It was cold now, but in ten minutes the desert would be warmed. In half an hour the rising sun would force all of them to throw back their hoods, and the broiling heat of a desert day would be upon them.

By noon, try how they would, Youba and Fedada had not been able to keep their cream-colored camel and the spindly-legged Amr'r at the head of the caravan. Amr'r had walked splendidly, but twice he had stopped to feed, gulping down his mother's rich milk — and all the time the rest of the camels had been marching by.

At the noon halt, when men spread their praying mats and bowed in the direction of Mecca for the seven-fold prayer, even Uncle Abbah was looking anxious. He had slowed down his ten camels so as not to leave Tamerouelt, Amr'r, and the two children behind.

While Youba and Fedada were getting food for the noon meal, one of the guards came along and spoke softly to Abbah. "The leader says that unless you can keep up with the rest of the caravan, you will have to kill the young camel."

"He will do better when he has had a rest," Abbah said confidently, in case Youba and Fedada could hear. But when he saw that they were still occupied, he shook his head and shrugged at the guard. "We will try, guard, for this young camel is the boy's first — a gift from his father, Moussa, who travels with the earlier caravan. You know how a boy feels about his first camel."

The guard nodded sympathetically. As he walked away he called over his shoulder: "The first camels are at a well up ahead. When it is your turn, let your beasts drink deep; there is no more water for forty miles. And remember — those who cannot keep pace usually end up feeding the vultures."

Fedada heard the guard's final words and looked worriedly at her brother, but Youba said nothing. He was afraid. Little Amr'r seemed too weary at this moment even to want to feed. Abbah, busy with a fraying rope, did not look up when Youba drew near to ask: "My uncle, is there nothing we can do for Amr'r? I think his legs are too stiff for him to walk much farther."

Abbah sucked in a sharp sighing breath, then slowly shook his head. "One can only hope that Allah will be merciful; but if Amr'r cannot walk — then I think it will mean a bullet from a guard's rifle."

"But couldn't we all stay behind with Amr'r?" Fedada asked as she handed her uncle a wooden bowl of millet and cheese. "If we walked just a little bit slower, we — "

Uncle Abbah was shaking his head. "Camel men travel in big caravans like this, Fedada, because it is the only safe way. What would your father think if, when we got to Timbuktu, we had lost all his ten camels, and the salt, and only had little Amr'r? No — we have got to keep up with the caravan."

Youba turned to stare at Amr'r. He had curled

up his thin legs, and his slender neck was stretched out on the hot sand. The thought of what would happen to him if he could not keep up with the caravan made Youba's heart feel cold. He looked anxiously along the line of camels, and wished that every one of them would drink deep at the well — for the longer they took, the more rest Amr'r could have.

THREE

A Friend
at the Right Time

As the line of camels drew nearer the well, Youba and Fedada passed a gray-haired old man squatting on the sand beside one of his two camels.

"The young camel is stiff," the old man called out to Youba. "You should put new life in his legs."

"New life?" Youba asked. "How does one do that, sir?"

Rising slowly, the old man went over to Amr'r who was now greedily taking a much-needed drink of his mother's milk. "Men call me Omar El Hassim," the man said proudly. "I am not a camel man, yet there are things I know about camels which many men born to caravan work do not know. Watch!"

While Youba and Fedada looked on, the old man began to stroke his long fingers down the muscles of Amr'r's spindly legs. What he was doing must

have been pleasant, for Amr'r, after only one at-
tempt at a kick, made no other protest. In fact,
after a minute or so his little tail began to wriggle
as a lamb's tail wriggles when it is feeding.

When Tamerouelt finally got to the well, and
drank her fill, she walked on to her place at the end
of the caravan. From now until the oven-heat of the
day was over no one would move. Old Omar made
sure his own camels were resting comfortably, then
came back to massage Amr'r's leg muscles some
more. Youba and Fedada watched in silence.

Their uncle joined them, and lighting a tiny fire,
made four glasses of sweet mint tea. Handing one

to the old man, he said, "This is something I would like to learn. Will it really put new life in the young camel's legs?"

"We shall know before the end of the day," Omar said, chuckling. He paused only for a few moments to drink the tea, then went on rubbing Amr'r's tired, stiff muscles.

Finally the dreaded moment came. From up at the head of the caravan a shot sounded. Men yelled to their camels. Grunting, snarling, and sounding thoroughly bad-tempered, the two hundred camels lurched to their feet — and one of them was Tamerouelt, and another was Amr'r.

Throughout the remainder of the afternoon Youba and Fedada walked alongside the baby. Twice he stopped to feed, yet after each feed he followed his mother, and somehow they were able to keep up with the tail end of the caravan. Only as the sun was beginning to set did Amr'r seem to suddenly tire and begin to lag. His feet dragged and they fell behind, so that by the time Tamerouelt, Amr'r, Youba, and Fedada arrived in the camp, the caravan had been halted, loads taken off the camels, and even a number of fires lit.

"Should we not join our uncle?" Fedada asked, when Tamerouelt sank to her knees at the end of the long line of camels. Youba looked at little Amr'r, who had folded his spindly legs even before his mother sank down to rest.

"I will go and seek him," Youba said. First, though, he glanced quickly to one side, and seeing Omar El Hassim, he whispered to his sister, "I want to stay here. The old man may be able to help Amr'r again if we are near."

Youba did not have far to go to find his uncle, for Abbah had got his ten camels settled, and leaving the servant to feed them, was coming to look for his nephew and niece.

"I am farther up the line," Abbah said. "A friend asked me to join with him. We will move Tamerouelt and her son to my campfire."

"My uncle, do you not think it would be better for us to stay at this end for an hour or so?" Youba suggested, pointing out that the old man who had massaged Amr'r was nearby and might do some more work on the young camel's tired muscles.

Abbah stroked his little beard for a moment, then agreed. "Come back for tea and food," he said, adding a word of caution: "I hope Amr'r will be strong for tomorrow. You must remember we are only at the beginning of the march."

Youba went with his uncle and collected fodder for Tamerouelt, as well as food and tea for him-

self and his sister. Fedada had already lit a small fire, taking a handful of prickly dry twigs from those stowed among the baggage Tamerouelt carried.

"Would you drink tea with us, sir?" Youba asked the old man, and Omar El Hassim's eyes twinkled as he accepted the invitation.

"I have few friends," he said, reaching for his bag of food, "and I have never had young friends. After we have eaten I will look at the young camel's legs again — and I will show you how to harden the pads of his feet. There is more than sand to be crossed before we reach Timbuktu. There are stony hills on which soft feet can easily be damaged."

While Fedada mixed pounded goat cheese and millet with water, Omar spent the time massaging Amr'r's muscles. With no fuss at all the little camel allowed itself to be turned round so that each of its long thin legs could benefit from the skill in the old man's fingers.

After they had eaten their gruel-like mixture of cheese and millet, Omar El Hassim said, "There is another thing to do for this young camel. Ahead is the pass of Foum El Alba. It is one of the roughest hill passes. Men tell me that more camels die in that pass than in any other place."

Youba and Fedada exchanged quick, troubled glances. They remembered the pass. On the way north from Timbuktu to the salt mines a big, splendidly built camel had slipped and broken a leg there. It had been put out of its misery with a rifle bullet. They did not want Amr'r to die like that.

"I will show you what to do," Omar said, and breaking off a piece of salt from one of the blocks his camel carried, he melted it in some of his precious drinking water. Then he tied rags soaked in the solution around each of Amr'r's foot pads.

While he was doing this, Abbah arrived, having threaded his way through the firelit gloom from the place where his camels were tethered for the night. He watched in silence while the salt-soaked pads were tied in place.

"Salt hardens the skin," old Omar explained. "If this is done each night, then perhaps this youngster's feet will not be injured when he has to walk among the sharp stones of the Foum El Alba pass."

"You are very kind to these children," Abbah said, saluting Omar. "Not every man would give of his salt and water for another man's camel."

"It is easy to be kind to children," the old man said. "A little salt and water costs no more than a man would give to a beggar, and giving of my wisdom is cheap when I see the joy in these young eyes. Now I go to sleep, for I am an old man. Allah be with you. Sleep well."

"Allah be with you also," Youba, Fedada, and Abbah said.

When the old man had lain down by the side of one of his camels, Abbah turned to Youba, saying, "Now, will you join me farther along the line?"

"Is it not better to let Tamerouelt and Amr'r stay here, my uncle?" Youba asked. "Amr'r has these salted rags about his feet. If he walks, they may come off."

Abbah considered for a moment, then nodded. "There is little danger here," he murmured. "But join me before we move on in the morning. Allah be with you and sleep well." The children returned his end-of-the-day wish, and Abbah strode off up the line.

The stars were shining like lamps in a sky clear of any sign of cloud. Tiny campfires twinkled, lighting up the bearded faces of camel men, and silhouetting the humped shapes of camels. Camels that had a tendency to stray were haltered by bending and then tying up the lower part of a forefoot.

For perhaps half an hour after their uncle had returned to his own camels, Youba and Fedada sat listening to the noises of the night. The burning heat of the day had gone with the setting of the sun. Now the air was quite cold, and everyone in the caravan had drawn the cowl of his garment over his head.

There was a murmur of conversation as men talked. At one fire a man was telling a story, and thirty or so men were gathered, their hawklike faces looking fierce in the flickering glow of the fire.

From much farther away came the sound of music, as a man played on a wooden instrument, producing music which sounded all the sweeter in the lonely wilderness of the desert.

Youba finally scooped sand over their little fire. The charred twigs would lie in the sand until morning, and would then light again without trouble. No man crossing the desert wasted even a twig, for every piece of wood had to be carried. Wood was precious.

The last fires died away and the last camel man scooped a hole in the sand and lay down. Then a deep silence fell over the caravan. After a hard day all was peace. As Youba dropped off to sleep, he was thinking gratefully of old Omar's kind actions — and fearfully of the long, dangerous route that still lay ahead of them all.

The sickle moon that rose over the desert an hour later cast a pale glow over the sleeping forms. Men and beasts slept soundly, for the first day's journey was always the hardest.

FOUR

In the Pass

In the days which followed there were many anxious moments for Youba and Fedada, and for their Uncle Abbah. Each morning they would start at the head of the caravan, but before the day ended they would be trailing at the rear. Uncle Abbah dropped back with them, but it was difficult for him, since he had ten laden camels to look to, and only one helper.

It was the old man, Omar El Hassim, who kept Amr'r going. When the caravan stopped at noon, he would immediately begin to stroke the young camel's tired muscles. He also persuaded Abbah to let him have a piece of salt. This he melted with water and soaked rags in the solution for Amr'r's feet. Slowly, yet certainly, the little camel began to improve. His muscles toughened, and his speed increased. There was less shouting from the guards. Then, on the tenth day, they began to climb the Foum El Alba pass. On that day Amr'r was walking as well at noon as in the coolness of the morning.

The pass was like a knife-slash through the hills. Jagged walls of rock towered on each side, and the way was littered with great slabs of rock which had fallen from above. In falling many of the rocks had shattered into a thousand pieces, and some of them had edges like a sword.

There was some confusion just after midday, for a camel had slipped and broken its neck. The guards would not allow the caravan to halt while the camel was skinned and its meat sold. They were now nearing the region where Moorish raiders from the Spanish Sahara might be encountered, and the pass would make a splendid place for an ambush.

Fedada turned her eyes away when they were passing the dead camel. Youba looked sadly at it and shook his head. It was the will of Allah that a camel should die like that, but it was a pity. It looked to have been a splendid beast.

A few minutes later, however, he had forgotten the dead camel, and was worrying about Amr'r. Stepping jauntily along, he had put his front right foot in among a clutter of pieces of shattered rock, and for the first time since he had been born the young camel squealed in pain.

A second later he almost fell, and then began to limp very badly, holding his foot off the ground. Youba called to Fedada who was riding Tamerouelt, and she wheeled the big she-camel around.

Slithering off Tamerouelt's back, she watched anxiously as her brother lifted Arm'r's right foot. Then her eyes widened with anguish as she saw drops of blood falling to the rocky floor of the pass. Amr'r had been injured.

There was nothing they could do then but bind up the foot, putting a pad of rag under the gash so that it would act as a cushion when Amr'r put his foot down.

Already the rear guard had come up and was urging them to hurry. "This is the worst place of all to stop," he shouted. "If the raiders happened to be on top of the rocks, they could shoot us down and no one would live to tell what had happened. Can he walk?"

"Oh, yes. Yes, he can walk," Youba said quickly. "We shall catch up with the caravan in a minute or so."

"Is that the truth?" Fedada asked, watching her brother tie the last knot on the rather rough bandage. "Surely Amr'r cannot walk well with such a pad on his foot."

"He will walk even worse if he does not have a pad," Youba said. "Come, mount Tamerouelt. Unless she is walking, Amr'r will not even try to follow."

For the next hour it was agony for Youba, Fedada, and Amr'r. The little camel showed that he came of the best camel stock the desert knew. Where an ordinary work camel would have snarled and protested, and finally slumped to his knees, little Amr'r kept on. He was in pain, but except for the limp he gave no sign of his suffering. No grunt or groan came from his tight-pressed lips.

Youba and Fedada were alone now with the two camels. Uncle Abbah was far ahead in the middle of the caravan, and even Omar El Hassim was out of sight. Youba thought of running ahead to seek help, but decided he couldn't risk leaving Fedada by herself. Suppose Amr'r stopped altogether, or the raiders came . . . ?

Suddenly Fedada pointed ahead, and Youba gave a deep sigh. Racing toward them on his magnificent milk-white mehari was the man in charge of the caravan guards.

"I suppose he will tell us to kill Amr'r," Youba muttered, stroking the top of the little camel's head. "Fedada, I can't do it. I can't let anyone do it. He is mine. The first camel I could ever call my own."

"And he is so beautiful," Fedada murmured. "Oh, my brother, what can we do?"

"I don't know." Youba watched anxiously as the armed man raced nearer, his camel moving so smoothly, and with such power. It was the kind of splendid animal Youba hoped Amr'r would grow into, if they did not kill him.

"You are holding up the caravan," the leader of the guard called out as he brought his camel to a stop with a single twitch of the rope in his right hand. "What is the matter? The camel is too tired to go farther, eh?"

"He has cut his front right foot pad on a stone," Youba said dejectedly.

"But it will soon heal," Fedada urged, her eyes showing her anxiety. "In an hour, maybe less — if he could just rest — the wound would heal, and then —"

She stopped, for the guard had swung down from his camel. Walking across to them, he lifted Amr'r's injured foot even higher off the gritty sand so that he could examine it.

One look was sufficient. The wound was not bleeding, but it was filled with sand. The rag had worked loose, and the cut must have been painful indeed.

Gently releasing Amr'r's injured foot, the hawk-faced man watched to see what the young camel would do. Amr'r put his foot gently on the ground, then lifted it again. That told the guard all he wanted to know: the foot was too painful to bear any weight at all.

"He will have to be shot," the guard said, looking at Youba, then at Fedada. "We cannot waste time waiting for an injured camel. Take the she-camel ahead and I'll deal with the young one."

Youba was stunned by the decision, even though he had been expecting it. He knew that the guards were in command of the caravan, and even the richest merchant had to obey them while on the march. Fedada, however, immediately put herself in front of Amr'r. "No . . . no . . . you can't shoot him!" she cried. "He *will* be all right soon, I know he will."

The guard stared at her as Youba blurted, "He is my very first camel. Please — give him another chance."

"You know there is a risk that we may be attacked," the guard said sternly. "We cannot afford to stop even for the best camel in the world."

"Give us just until tomorrow," Youba begged. "If he is not fit to walk then . . ." But he could not finish what he meant to say.

"I'll see if we can halt the caravan a little earlier . . . at the foot of the pass," the guard said in a gentler voice. "But you must hurry if you are to catch up before sunset. And remember—this is your responsibility. I cannot guarantee your safety."

"Yes, sir," Youba said.

"If his foot is not healed by tomorrow," the guard added, swinging up onto his camel, "you will come and tell me, and allow him to be shot."

Fedada turned and stroked Amr'r's shapely head. Youba nodded. To allow his first camel to be shot would be the hardest thing he had ever done, yet he knew he would have to do it if Amr'r could not walk.

A moment later the guard had swung his beautiful mehari around and was on his way back to the caravan. Already the last camels were several hundred yards ahead.

As he rode off, Youba dropped to his knees to examine once again Amr'r's injured foot. At sight of it he groaned. Walking had opened the wound and across the soft pad ran a gaping slash. It could not possibly heal by morning, and the more the little camel walked, the more sand would be ground into the cut.

"I shall pray to Allah," Fedada said as Youba undid the crumpled rag and retied it in an effort to keep out the glistening, diamond-hard grains of sand.

"I, too, shall pray," Youba said quietly, but he knew that only a miracle could save Amr'r.

"Allah Helps Those Who Help Themselves"

The sun had set when Amr'r finally limped to the end of the resting caravan. The Foum El Alba pass lay two miles behind them, and the little camel was drooping. He had limped bravely on, but the effort had taken all his strength. Now, the moment Youba halted Tamerouelt, Amr'r sank down, his long thin legs doubled under him, his neck outstretched so that his head could rest on the sand.

Tiny campfires flickered in the starlit gloom, and men whispered to one another as they prepared their food and tea. There had been light-hearted talk and laughter on the other evenings, and Youba felt there must be something wrong tonight. Leaving his sister to light a small fire and prepare food, he hurried along the line of resting camels until he came upon his uncle, the servant, and their ten camels.

"Allah be praised," Abbah said, clasping Youba to him. "Where is your sister? Is she safe?"

"She is at the end of the line with Tamerouelt and Amr'r," Youba said. "We were late. Amr'r cut his foot —"

"Yes, I know. A guard told me, and refused to let me drop behind to help. They are afraid of trouble. One of our guards who always rides ahead saw a rider when he reached the foot of the pass. They fear he may be a scout for a band of those accursed raiders. The caravan will start at first light tomorrow. Tell me, how well can the young camel walk?"

Youba only shrugged. He could imagine what his uncle would say when he saw Amr'r's injury. Like most men of the desert his uncle prized camels. Yet if the safety of his nephew and niece, or the caravan, should be at stake, he would not hesitate to kill Amr'r, or insist that he be left behind.

"My uncle," Youba said as they drew near the end of the line of camels. "You are a man with great experience of camels. I am sure you will be able to make Amr'r's foot right. How can I see him shot? He is my first camel — my father's gift."

"I know," his uncle said gruffly. "And a man's first camel is always precious. May he live to carry you many journeys across the sand."

Yet when they came on the two camels, with the

little fire still flickering nearby, Youba's uncle took one long, careful look at Amr'r's injured foot and shook his head.

"He will never manage the rest of the journey," he announced. "I will kill him now, and we can sell the meat to —"

"No!" the protest came from Fedada, and rising from the fire, she stood between her uncle and Amr'r. "You cannot kill him now, my uncle. By tomorrow the foot may have healed."

"That is girl's talk," her uncle said rather crossly. "Have I not worked with camels all my life? I *know* when an injury is too bad to heal quickly. A few days would see him walking quite well — but as I have already told your brother, the caravan will move at dawn." And brushing back his outer garment he was in the act of drawing his knife from its sheath when Youba, his face puckered in a troubled frown, said:

"Uncle, let us leave it until dawn. If he cannot walk — then he shall be killed."

"But if you kill him now his meat could be sold. The other camel men would buy it all. They are hungry for meat."

"No!" The thought of little Amr'r being cut up for the cooking pot sent a cold chill of horror through Youba.

Seeing the look on his nephew's face, Uncle Abbah relented. "Then bring them both along to my fire," he said. "I have food ready and —"

"Thank you, Uncle," Youba interrupted with a relieved sigh. "But Fedada is already preparing food, and Amr'r is so weary we would like to let him stay here. If he can keep his injured foot off the sand, it might heal quicker."

"It will not heal by tomorrow," Abbah said soberly. "I think it would be better if you made up your mind now that he just cannot go on. I have been worried every day about you. Did I not promise your father that I would care for you, and now —"

"But you have, my uncle," Youba broke in hurriedly. "No one could have done more. Let us have this last chance, please. I promise that if Amr'r cannot walk tomorrow, then . . ."

Abbah sat down and rubbed thoughtfully at his beard. He was very worried. There was a real risk now that the caravan would be attacked, and he wanted his brother's children to be with him if that did happen. Yet when he saw Youba's determined expression and the hope in Fedada's eyes, he could not bring himself to insist that the young camel be killed there and then.

Rising, he said sternly: "You must come to me

the moment men begin to move tomorrow. If the young camel cannot walk, then you will leave him behind. You will promise that, my nephew! And, Fedada, you will see that your brother keeps the promise."

"Yes, Uncle!" Both Youba and Fedada had to make that promise, for they knew their uncle was responsible for them.

After Uncle Abbah had left, Youba sank down by Fedada's fire, and stared beyond the flickering flames into the night. There seemed no hope at all for little Amr'r.

It would not have been so bad if the young camel had groaned and whined at the pain, or had had to be kept moving by blows. But none of that had happened. Amr'r had given one cry only, when the sharp-edged rock had slashed his foot. From then on he had limped along in silence. Even when weariness had made his proud little head begin to droop, he had struggled on.

Fedada poured tea into a little glass and handed it to Youba. "Drink, my brother," she coaxed. "I have been praying to Allah, and I am sure he will listen to my prayers. He will not let Amr'r die."

Youba took the glass and looked across the top of it at his sister. Fedada's dark eyes were pleading with him not to give way to despair; yet he knew there was no hope. Amr'r could not keep pace with the other camels, nor would their uncle let them lag behind with him. They must travel with the rest of the caravan.

They ate their meal of pounded millet and dried goat cheese in silence, but as they were finishing they had a visitor. It was the old man, Omar El Hassim. He came up quietly, gave them a salute, then sat cross-legged by their fire. When Fedada apologized for not being able to offer him a glass of the mint-flavored tea, he smiled. "I did not come for tea, but to apologize to *you* for not dropping behind to help you this afternoon. My camels were nervous in the pass and hard to control; I had to stay close by them."

Youba and Fedada nodded, and after a short silence Omar El Hassim said, "I heard from the guard about the young camel's injury and have brought two things which may help him. Bring Amr'r over to the fire so that I may take a look at his foot."

They coaxed Amr'r to his feet, then forced him to lie down by the side of the fire. Omar El Hassim brought out a needle threaded with a fine thread, which he said he had used before for tasks like this.

While Fedada and Youba held Amr'r's leg the old man cleaned the wound of sand, using some of his own precious water to do it. Then from a small cardboard box he took a paste which he smeared over the cut. After that he stitched the edges of the wound together.

Youba and Fedada exchanged glances, wondering why Amr'r did not kick. Guessing what they were thinking, the old man explained: "Though this Amr'r is young, the skin of his foot pads was thick at birth. He feels no pain from the needle. Allah

gave every camel big soft feet so that they would not sink in the sand. He also gave their feet thick skin so that the heat would not burn them. And he gave them courage. Some he gave more courage than others. Amr'r was one to whom he gave great courage."

"And will the foot be healed by morning?" Youba asked doubtfully. "My uncle, who has been a camel man all his life, said —"

"The foot will not be healed," the old man interrupted. "But if it is well wrapped, then sand will not get into the wound, and Amr'r may walk."

"But will he be able to walk as quickly as the rest of the camels?" Youba wanted to believe Amr'r would be all right, yet deep down in his heart he knew that the little camel would limp for days.

Omar El Hassim leaned back, smiling. "Long ago, when I was in great trouble like you, I went to a holy man — a *Marabout* — for help. He told me: 'When you are in trouble, pray to Allah, but always remember that Allah helps those who help themselves.' He was a very wise man.

"It is not for me, an old man, to tell you what to do," Omar El Hassim said gently. "You are young, and strong, and you love this baby camel. If you think, perhaps an idea will come to you. What I can do is tell you that the way ahead is not as difficult as the way through the pass. Only a fool could get lost, the guards tell me. For hours the track lies between soft sand dunes. It is a natural valley. If someone was foolish enough to climb the dunes, then he could get lost. But not otherwise."

He sighed and rose slowly to his feet. "Now I will go, for I am tired. I will look at the young camel's foot at sunset tomorrow. With more of this ointment smeared into the cut, and a rag to keep the sand from the wound, I am sure he will walk with you into Timbuktu in a few weeks' time. Allah stay with you. Sleep well."

He ambled away, leaving Youba and Fedada to watch him in silence.

"Why did he say only a fool could get lost on the way ahead?" Youba said at length.

Fedada shook her head. She thought she knew, but she was afraid to say.

Youba looked at his sister for a long moment, then said, "I think I know what he was trying to tell us."

"Yes?" There was a suggestion of a quiver in Fedada's voice.

"Did he not say that Allah helped those who help themselves? We could help ourselves. *We* could save Amr'r. Suppose we started south — before dawn?"

"But we couldn't," Fedada protested, and now there was fear in her voice. "You heard what our uncle said about the raiders."

"Will they attack before there is any light?" Youba asked. "Even these Moorish robbers need some light to see. We could start in the false dawn, before the real one, and perhaps save Amr'r that way."

"Did we not promise our uncle that —"

"We promised that if Amr'r could not walk, we would leave him behind," Youba said quickly. "But if Amr'r *can* walk, then we might save him by starting before everyone else."

"I am afraid," Fedada said.

"I thought you wanted to help Amr'r," Youba said scornfully. "Is that the way to save my first camel? Must he die because you are afraid?"

Fedada blinked in an effort to keep back tears, but they overflowed onto her cheeks.

"All right, we will not do it," Youba said, putting an arm around his sister's shoulders. "If you are so frightened, then —"

"I am frightened," Fedada interrupted, "but for Amr'r's sake I will do it."

SIX

A Sound
Beyond the Dunes

Rising, Youba took Amr'r back to Tamerouelt. He had earlier haltered the big she-camel by tying up one of her forelegs. This prevented her from wandering off in the moonlight to look for the occasional prickly shrubs on which camels delight to graze.

When he returned to their little fire Fedada had dried her tears, but she was worried now about something else, and asked doubtfully, "My brother, how shall we wake up in time to lead Tamerouelt and Amr'r south? You know that when I sleep I do not waken until the sun is shining."

"That is because you are only a woman," Youba said, smiling in a rather superior way. "We men can keep watch. You shall sleep, but I shall stay awake."

"If you stay awake, then I also shall stay awake

part of the time," Fedada insisted. "And while you are sleeping I will prepare food for the first meal of the day."

Youba finally agreed to his sister sharing the night watches with him. Already some of the little fires were being put out. The camel men went to sleep early, for the days were very tiring. Besides, wood for fires was so scarce they could not afford to sit talking long around a campfire.

Fedada scooped out a hollow in the sand. That was her bed for the night. Though the air was now quite cold, neither she nor Youba had any blankets. She wrapped herself in her clothing, pulled her hood well over her head, and in a minute or so was sound asleep.

Youba did not lie down. Had he done so he, too, would soon have been as sound asleep as his sister. He sat staring down the line of the caravan until the last red point of light went out as the final campfire was extinguished. There was an occasional grunt from a camel, but even these sounds faded, and the night was completely silent.

No wind stirred, and after a little while Youba had the feeling that he was the only person alive in the desert. In the east a quarter moon rose, and its light gave a silvery sheen to the sand dunes. The camels, sitting in little circles, heads together, looked like black carvings. Their masters sprawled nearby were like shapeless bundles of rags. The four guards left on watch were huddled against their camels for warmth.

Remembering that when a camel is wakened it usually protests with an angry snarl, or by making a hoarse gurgling sound, Youba prepared two gags. These were strips of cloth which he would tie around the muzzles of both Amr'r and Tamerouelt. If they could not open their mouths, then neither baby nor mother could utter a sound.

"We must move off silently," he told himself. "For if the men of this caravan fear raiders, their sleep will be uneasy, and the least sound will waken them. If they waken, and see us, they will not let us go off alone."

He had no watch, but he could measure the night by the way the moon made its way across the cloudless sky. Around midnight, when Fedada had been asleep for a little over three hours, he awakened her. Whispering, he told her to waken him when the moon reached a certain point over the towering dunes, then he lay down.

Before the false dawn, that strange light which spreads across the horizon about half an hour before the real dawn comes, Fedada awakened her brother. She had kept watch for almost six hours.

When Youba protested that she should have awakened him much earlier, she smiled and said, "My brother, I have been busy. Not only have I prepared food that we can eat now, but I have prepared food for later."

"But I have had twice as much sleep as you," Youba protested. "You will be too tired to walk, and —"

"You are forgetting something," Fedada interrupted. "Yesterday, and each day since we started out for Timbuktu, I have ridden part of the way on Tamerouelt. You have not ridden at all. Am I not your sister? Should I not care for you?"

"You are a better sister than I deserve," Youba said, and sat down to eat. Neither spoke now. Both were worrying. Suppose one of the camels made a sound! If the caravan was disturbed, and both men and beasts slept more lightly with the approach of morning, then all their plans could be upset.

Youba muzzled Tamerouelt, struggling as the big she-camel rose swiftly to protest. Yet the rag was wound about her muzzle before she was really awake, and she could neither snarl nor gurgle. Little Amr'r was sleeping as soundly as any baby, and he was muzzled before he realized what was happening.

While Youba was doing this, Fedada was fastening their few belongings onto Tamerouelt — their water bag, their food, kettle, spoons, and the dish in which they mixed their cheese and millet. There was also a small bag of dates. Then they were ready.

They had taken longer than they expected, and already the tips of the sand dunes were visible, outlined by the first signs of the false dawn showing on the distant horizon.

Taking Tamerouelt's lead rope, Youba started to walk her away from the caravan. Amr'r wanted to feed, but this would have to come later. The dunes

began about a hundred yards away, and Youba had decided they would walk along the foot of the dunes, parallel to the sleeping caravan. In this way there was less chance of being seen or heard by the caravan guards.

Fedada led little Amr'r, and the silence was the silence of a world that is completely dead. No insects buzzed. There was no breath of wind to sigh among the dunes. The only sound was the soft, very soft swish-swish-swish of their camels' feet.

They had gone about fifty yards when Youba

dragged Tamerouelt to a stop. In the darkness ahead he had heard something. It was no more than the tink of metal on metal; yet there should not have been any sound from the dunes. Fedada had also heard the noise, and halted Amr'r.

Both youngsters were straining to catch another sound, and their hearts were beating rapidly. No one from the caravan was out there beyond the dunes. What or who had made that sound: the *tink* of metal on metal?

Then, in the brooding silence, they heard a more familiar noise — the soft swish-swish-swish which camels make on sand. Someone, no, more than one, was drawing nearer. What was more, the camels were moving very slowly, which was a strange thing at this moment between night and day. Men who marched through the night moved as quickly as their camels could walk. People who moved quietly were people who did not wish to be heard!

Youba suddenly remembered what the men had talked about around their campfires — the raiders. The fierce Moorish men who came from the Spanish Sahara. Raiders on swift camels. Raiders who swept in to attack caravans at the first gray of dawn; killing if there was any resistance, robbing, and sometimes leaving the camel men without a beast to ride or water to drink.

Youba spun around to face the way they had just come. Unseen in the gloom, not more than fifty yards away, men and beasts were sleeping. Among them were his uncle and the gentle old man, Omar El Hassim. Were they to die by a raider's bullet? With a wild, piercing cry, Youba gave the alarm. His cry shattered the quiet.

"Wake! WAKE! W A K E! The raiders are here!"

SEVEN

Disaster at Dawn

Within seconds of Youba's alarm the night was hideous with a variety of wild, frightening sounds. Camels gurgled and snarled as they rose. Men shouted, and from the darkness of the sand dunes, where that telltale swish of camels' feet had first warned Youba and Fedada that strangers were about, came something else: the darkness was slashed by sudden stabs of flame, and the frightening *crack-crack-crack* of rifles.

The raiders added to the pandemonium with shrieks and yells as they spurred their camels on in a charge. They had not meant to attack the caravan until the real dawn gave them enough light to shoot by. Now, in the hope of frightening the caravan men into running away, they fired and yelled as they charged forward.

A bullet passed so close to Youba's left ear that he ducked, for the sound was like that of an angry bee buzzing by. A moment later Tamerouelt reared on her hind legs; she dragged Youba upward until he was on tiptoe, the halter rope twisted about his wrist pulling as tight as a straining hawser.

He gasped with the pain of it, for his wrist felt as if it had been squeezed by some giant hand, while the jerk on his shoulder muscles was even more painful. A moment later he was being forced to run. Taking giant strides, the she-camel turned aside and with her long legs carrying her over the ground at more than ten miles an hour, she dragged Youba after her.

Even above the uproar, Youba heard his sister scream. Terror at all the noise, coupled with the urge to follow his mother, helped Amr'r forget the pain of his injured foot, and young though he was, Fedada could not hold the baby camel back. Like Youba, she had wrapped the halter rope about her wrist, and unable to release it, was yanked after the young camel.

Youba was fleet-footed and might have been able to keep pace with Tamerouelt, but after she had raced along for about two hundred yards, she swung her head to one side. The sudden jolt on the rope threw Youba off balance. He stumbled and fell. Tamerouelt dragged him for a dozen yards

through the soft sands at the foot of the dunes, then
the rope came free from Youba's aching wrist.

Fedada had already been forced to loosen the

rope about her wrist, and that gave Amr'r the chance to follow his mother. In the gray light of the false dawn, mother and son raced away.

"Youba ... YOUBA!"

Youba, lying face down on the cold sand, his lungs crying out for air, his shoulder and right wrist aching almost more than he could bear, heard his sister screaming his name.

"Here ... Here!" he managed to shout, and Fedada heard him.

"Where are you, my brother?" Fedada was crying with anxiety, and when she did find Youba she clutched his hand and held it while tears streamed down her face.

She was very frightened. Back in the stretch of flat desert where the caravan had spent the night, there was a continuing hubbub. Camels were roaring; men were shouting. The raiders were firing rifles, and the caravan guards were shooting back.

Youba and Fedada sat huddled together. In the first wild rush with Tamerouelt and Amr'r they had come around the base of a dune and could see nothing, even though the real dawn was now beginning to make the stars look a little paler. The full light of a new day would be there in another ten minutes, but they could see neither the caravan nor the raiders because of the huge sand dune behind them.

"We . . . shall stay . . . here," Youba gasped, holding his sister tight. "When the raiders have been beaten off . . . we can go down and see if our uncle is safe."

The shooting grew less frequent as the new day dawned, and finally, after they had been there almost twenty minutes, only an occasional faraway shot was heard. Youba wanted to go and see what was happening, but Fedada clung to him. "A few more minutes will make no difference, my brother," she pleaded. "Wait just a little while. When there is no more shooting, then it will be safe."

They waited another four or five minutes, and during most of that time there was no sound at all. Finally Youba rose and went cautiously around the foot of the sand dune. He had to walk about two hundred yards before he could see the level patch where the caravan had spent the night.

In silence he stood and stared. Everything was changed. He could see several camels, but they were not kneeling. They were stretched out, and he knew at once that they were dead. There were odds and ends scattered along the path where the caravan had spent the night — little pieces of equipment, left when the camel men loaded in a hurry and rushed south for safety. They were all gone; camels, owners, and guards. There did not seem to be a man left.

Silently Youba returned to Fedada and told her the caravan had gone. Either they had escaped, or the raiders had captured the whole caravan and had marched it away.

"And we are alone?" Fedada said, her lower lip quivering.

"We'll look for Tamerouelt and Amr'r," Youba said, trying not to let his anxiety show in his voice. "At least you packed food and water on Tamerouelt, so we shall be all right."

Fedada gave him a quick sideways glance, and nodded. She knew as well as her brother that they would not be "all right." They had crossed this desert only once, from south to north, and things looked different when you were going in the opposite direction. How could they possibly find their way from water hole to water hole?

Youba guessed what she was thinking, and tried to comfort her. "We have only to keep marching south, and we'll reach Timbuktu."

Again Fedada nodded, but she knew it would not be as easy as that. They were a long way from Timbuktu. They had food for maybe three days, water for no more than two days. If they did not discover one of the small water holes, then they would die. The nearest oasis, where there were palm trees, mud-brick houses, and people who would give them food, was Araouane. And both of them had heard their uncle say that it was at least several days' march to the south.

EIGHT

"We Are Lost!"

"We'll track the camels," Youba announced, refusing to think of the terrible dangers ahead. "I think Tamerouelt must have been wounded by a bullet. She gave a tremendous leap when the first shots were fired. I have never known her to do anything like that before, and she has heard gunfire many times."

Fedada closed her eyes for a moment at the thought of added trouble. If the she-camel was wounded, perhaps dying, how could they feed Amr'r? How could they carry their water and food, kettle, cooking pan? She said nothing, but followed Youba who was now looking for the tracks of Tamerouelt and Amr'r.

It was midmorning before they found the two camels. Tamerouelt had well earned her name which meant "The Hare." She had raced across the dunes toward the foot of the Foum El Alba pass, and had only stopped when she realized that her young son was not with her.

Terror and bewilderment had sent Amr'r racing after his mother, and enabled him to forget the pain in his foot for the few minutes of the mad rush. When the two children reached the spot where the camels were, Amr'r had loosened his gag, consoled himself with a long, long drink of milk, and was now lying down. He had suffered no additional injury.

Somehow Tamerouelt had managed to get rid of the rag which had been tied about her muzzle, and when Youba reached her the big she-camel was browsing on a prickly thorn bush growing about two feet high through the sand. It looked as appetizing as a pincushion or a porcupine, yet she seemed to be enjoying her meal, despite the fact that the sharp prickles had drawn blood from her lips.

Youba could see no sign of a wound until he went around to her right side. Then his eyes widened for a moment in alarm. Dried blood darkened her chest and one leg. Cautiously he rubbed the dried blood away, and finally discovered the bullet wound. At sight of it he breathed a great sigh of relief.

"It is only a graze," he called to Fedada, who was on her knees examining Amr'r's injured foot. "It looks no more than a cut. She won't die, I'm sure."

Despite his optimism, when they tried to lead

Tamerouelt back to the place where the caravan had been attacked, the big she-camel limped very badly. The bullet, though it had caused no more than a flesh wound, had badly bruised the muscles, and they had stiffened.

Youba managed to coax Tamerouelt to walk, but progress was so slow that the sun was at high noon before they rounded the last tall hill of sand and came in sight of the place where they had camped the night before. There was more evidence now that a battle had been fought.

Vultures were flying in to feast on the dead camels. There were at least thirty of the ugly-looking scavengers already at work, and more were winging their way down.

As Youba and Fedada marched the limping Tamerouelt and the equally limping Amr'r along the flat, silent land where a few hours before there had been shooting and shouting, there was plenty of evidence that the caravan had fled in haste. Used cartridge cases shone in the brilliant sunshine. There was a little green teapot lying by the side of two glasses, left there the night before so that their owner would be able to make his morning tea without much trouble.

There was even a gerba, and Youba gave a shout when he saw it; but the goatskin water bag con-

tained only a little water. It had been abandoned because a bullet had struck it, and practically all the water had leaked away into the hot sand.

Suddenly, as they walked along, Fedada called anxiously, "My brother, there is a kneeling camel ahead, and no vultures there. He must be alive, but why has he stayed here?"

Youba had already seen the big, sand-colored camel. He handed Tamerouelt's halter rope to Fedada and went over to see whether the camel was seriously wounded, perhaps dying, or whether there was some other reason why it had not rushed off when the caravan fled south.

As he drew near he called to it to rise, and the big beast did begin to rise, only to have its head jerked down, so that it was forced to sink to its knees again. At the same time a croaking voice called, "Allah be praised. I thought I was going to stay here until the sun roasted me and I died of thirst. Come around, friend, for I have a bullet through my leg."

Youba hurried to see where the voice came from, and gaped in amazement when he saw Omar El Hassim lying with his back to a dead camel, and keeping the other one kneeling by a firm grip on its headrope.

"Fedada, come quickly," Youba called; bending down, he tried to lift the old man to his feet.

"No, no, let me sit. When I move, the world and the sky begin to turn round and round," Omar gasped. "I have a bullet through the lower part of my leg. It does not bleed now — but I am so dried-up for want of water that I am faint. Can you give me a drink?"

While Fedada went to get their gerba of water, Omar looked hard at Youba. "Where were the two of you when the raiders came? I didn't see you anywhere."

"We woke early and started ahead with Amr'r," Youba replied. "It was your words last night that gave us the idea. And we were the ones who heard the raiders. I shouted the alarm —"

"Praise Allah for that," old Omar sighed, leaning back on his elbows. "But if any harm had come to you because of what I said — if the raiders had captured you — I could never have forgiven myself."

"No, it was my doing, not yours. All I could think of was saving Amr'r." A shudder went through Youba as he thought of what might have happened in those terrible moments between the false and the real dawn.

Just then Fedada returned with their precious water supply. There was no more than four pints, and she was frowning as Youba held the mouth of the gerba to Omar El Hassim's lips. She had heard it said that a wounded man always cried out for water — and this was the only water they had.

Omar drank sparingly. Then, holding the neck of the gerba so that not a drop could leak out, he asked, "How much water have you besides this?"

It was an easy question to answer. "That is all the water we have," Youba said quietly. "But drink. You have had no more than a mouthful."

The old man put the gerba to his lips, then took it away again. There was a husky kind of chuckle in his voice when he said, "I am going to tell a lie, but I know Allah will forgive me. Take the gerba away, for I am no longer thirsty."

"But you were fainting for water," Youba reminded him. "Drink a little more."

"Only a little, then," Omar El Hassim agreed, "for perhaps in a day even that drop will seem like a gift from Allah."

"Forgive me for disagreeing with you, sir," Youba said apologetically. "I am only a boy, and you are a man whose white hairs tell of age and wisdom, but have you forgotten our uncle? When he discovers that we are not with the caravan he will surely come back to look —" He stopped, for Omar El Hassim was shaking his head.

"You are a boy, but already almost a man in wisdom," the old man said gravely. "So I am going to tell you the truth. Your uncle *will not come back for you.*"

"That is hard to believe, sir," Youba protested. "Our uncle, who is my father's younger brother, is a good man. He would not leave me and my sister to die of thirst in this waterless land."

Again Omar El Hassim shook his head as he explained: "I lay here pretending to be dead when the caravan had gone, for the raiders came looking for loot. They are a wild, lawless band. Some were wounded, and they had no plunder to reward them for all the weeks they have spent crossing the desert from Spanish Sahara."

"But they —" Youba began eagerly, only to stop as Omar El Hassim lifted a hand for silence.

"What I am trying to explain," he said gently, "is that these raiders are empty-handed. Your uncle could not get back here, for he would surely meet them. And if he did, they would kill him and take all he had — camels, food, water, everything."

"But he will still try to come back," Youba insisted. "Even though he risks his life. Our uncle loves us, and —"

"The guards will not let him," Omar El Hassim interrupted weakly. "Each man with camels in the caravan paid toward the wages of the guards. Each man also agreed to obey the orders of the guard leader. What I tell you is the truth. Your uncle will not come back. So do not expect his help."

There followed a long moment of frightened silence and then the old man said, "Had you not given the alarm, few of the caravan men would have got away. As it was, the guards began shooting at once. That made the raiders halt their charge, and it gave us the chance to load our camels. I think I fainted from the shock of the bullet, and the others must have thought I was dead."

There was another pause before the old man went on. "The caravan will hurry south as fast as they can go, for they will expect the raiders to follow and attack again. That is why I am sure no one will come back to look for you."

Youba drew in a long, deep breath. He knew his sister was looking anxiously at him, waiting for him to speak. Omar El Hassim was also waiting. For the first time in his life Youba was the only one who could decide what must be done. His heart was beating wildly against his ribs, but he said as bravely as he could, "Then we must start south and make the journey alone. We will put you on your camel, sir. Perhaps we can catch up with the caravan."

"With a wounded camel, and a young camel with an injured foot?" Omar El Hassim asked, shaking his head slowly. "We could not hope to do it. How far is the next water hole? One day — two, maybe three days?"

Youba frowned and shook his head. "That I do not know, sir. Fedada and I crossed this desert for the first time when we came north with our father and uncle some weeks ago. Our father did keep telling me to make careful note of everything I saw, but who can remember a trackless way after only one journey?"

"No, not after half a dozen journeys," was Omar's reply.

"But *you* will know the way, sir," Fedada put in eagerly. "A man with so many years behind him will know the desert as a camel knows how to drink enough water for a week."

To the surprise and dismay of both Youba and Fedada, Omar El Hassim shook his head.

"I was born in Timbuktu," he explained. "As a boy I crossed the desert to the salt mines of Taoudenni. That was almost fifty years ago. I have never crossed the desert since, and am crossing it now only because I am too old to work. You see, I was returning to my birthplace to spend the rest of my days there. I do not know the way. Nor do I know where the water holes are."

Youba swallowed hard. "If *you* do not know the way, and *I* do not know the way then . . . then . . . " He hesitated to finish the sentence.

Omar El Hassim finished it for him. "Then — we are lost. Yes, that is true. And that is why, though I am thirsty, I drank so little water. We are lost, and the nearest water hole may be days ahead. How many days, or where exactly it is, not one of us knows."

NINE

Following
the Caravan Tracks

All three sat staring at each other until Fedada abruptly rose to her feet. "I shall light a small fire and make tea with the water we have left," she said briskly to Omar. "While the water is boiling I will look to your wound and my brother can search where the caravan rested, in case someone has left behind a gerba of water, or anything else which might be useful. Is that a good idea?"

Youba looked in astonishment at his sister. Among desert people it was not the custom for girls to make suggestions when things of importance were being spoken of. Perhaps the old man would think Fedada impudent. He was relieved when Omar El Hassim chuckled approvingly and said, "Boy, you have a sister who talks with the wisdom of a man. Do you agree with what she says?"

Youba could only nod, and he wandered off to

search each of the tiny campsites in case something
of value had been left behind. Fedada examined the
bullet wound in Omar El Hassim's leg. They could
not spare water to wash the wound, but when she
looked inquiringly at the old man he said, "It is a
clean wound. The bullet went right through. Bind
it with a rag. In a week or ten days it will have
healed."

Since he did not seem too worried about it, Fedada did as he suggested, tearing a strip of cloth
from the bottom of her dress to use as a bandage.
Then she lit a fire and carefully drained every drop
of water from the gerba into their kettle. She was
dismayed to discover how little water they had.

By the time the tea had been made, Youba was
back. He carried a gerba, a small sack of millet,
some dates, and a bundle of provender for their
camels. As he laid the gerba down he said trium-
phantly: "We are lucky. There is sufficient water
here for another day, perhaps even longer if we are
careful."

He sat down and watched Fedada pour the tea.
After they had finished drinking, and Fedada had
carefully cleaned the glasses with sand, Youba said,
"I think we should start south, now, sir. If we follow the tracks of the caravan they will surely lead
us to the next water hole. Since you are injured and

cannot walk, we will put our food and the gerba on Tamerouelt, which my sister will ride. You can ride your own camel. I will walk. It will be no hardship, for I have walked since we left Taoudenni."

"And my salt?" the old man asked. "What of that? Allah be praised, the raiders must have thought it not worth halting for my poor baggage. Yet those six blocks are all I have. They cannot be left behind."

"The salt must be left behind, sir," Youba said firmly. "We have only the two camels. Can your camel carry you *and* the salt? It would be too much, and I know Tamerouelt cannot carry your salt and my sister."

"I could walk," Fedada suggested timidly.

"No. Even if you walked, the salt would be too heavy for her. Not only is she limping, but she is also feeding Amr'r. You could not expect her to have the strength to do so many things. The salt must be left."

"No! That will only be left behind if I stay behind." There was no gentleness in Omar El Hassim's voice now. "If I had a son in Timbuktu who would offer me a corner in his house, and give me food, then I would leave the salt. But there is no one to welcome me to the place where I was born. If I leave my salt behind — then I shall return to

Timbuktu a penniless beggar. I could not face a life of sitting at the street corner, begging from those who pass by."

"But we can only take you if you ride Tamerouelt, and your own camel carries the salt," Youba protested. "That would mean my sister would have to walk. If we do this we may never reach the next water hole. You must know, sir, that even a little wind can blow sand into footprints. Tracks that are a day or so old can be lost forever. Is it not better to leave the salt than stay here to die?"

Omar El Hassim turned to Fedada, and there was a wistful note in his voice when he said, "Fedada, you will not leave me, I know. I have seen goodness in your eyes from the first day I looked on you. Speak to your brother. Allah is good. He will see that the tracks to the water hole remain to guide us. You will not leave an old man to die alone in this sand."

Fedada turned to her brother, but Youba was angry. He grabbed the riding saddle lying by the side of Tamerouelt and swung it on her creamy back. Without looking at the old man he said angrily, "There are three laws for those who walk the desert, sir. One—you must see that your camel is strong and drinks his fill of water before you leave the oasis. The second law is that you must carry a full gerba for yourself; and the third is that you must know where the next water hole lies. We cannot keep any of those laws. We have one good camel, and three people. If I had not found this gerba, we would have no water at all now. And most important, we do not know where the next water hole lies."

"But if we follow the tracks of the caravan," Fedada urged, "they will lead us to water."

"We might do that if we leave the six slabs of salt behind," Youba said sharply. "For then you could ride Tamerouelt — and you are not heavy. Omar El Hassim could ride his camel, and so we might hurry, before the wind rises and wipes out the tracks."

"Then you will not take me," the old man said gently.

"Only a fool would take you!" The anger in Youba's voice made it rise almost to a shout. He was going to say more, but his glance rested for a second on Amr'r. He was feeding, taking his mother's rich milk in long, greedy sucks. Then Youba remembered how much Omar El Hassim had done for the baby camel. He had saved Amr'r not once but several times.

Suddenly Youba was ashamed. Turning to the old man, he said, "Sir, perhaps I am a fool, but I cannot leave you here. Come, my sister, help me lift him on Tamerouelt's back. It means you will have to walk all the time."

"I can do that," Fedada said. "Allah will repay you, my brother, I know he will."

They helped Omar El Hassim onto Tamerouelt, then loaded the six slabs of salt onto the old man's camel. It was a mangy-looking beast, and twice it tried to bite Youba as he tightened the ropes which held the slabs of salt in place.

"Strike it hard on the nose," the old man suggested. "That is the way to show you are its master."

Youba grunted, but did not strike the camel. He called both beasts to their feet, and the march south began. They passed a place where vultures were feeding on one of the salt camels that had died from a stray bullet. Fedada screwed up her face in disgust as the horrible-looking birds of prey flapped noisily into the air, only to return to their feasting as soon as the two adult camels and little Amr'r had gone by.

Through the rest of the sun-scorched day they walked steadily south. Youba had to slow down Omar's camel, for Tamerouelt was limping badly

and could not keep up. Little Amr'r, too, needed attention. The rag on his injured foot kept working loose, and Fedada grew quite expert at retying it.

Only the big, raw-boned working camel protested when they stopped to allow Amr'r to feed. And once the salt-laden beast had flopped to the sand he did not want to get up again. It was slow going all day, and their speed was less than two miles an hour.

Toward sundown, when Fedada was almost too weary to continue, there was a sudden gust of hot wind which stirred up a fog of sand for a minute or so. The wind died down almost at once, but it made Fedada, Youba, and Omar El Hassim turn and look worriedly to the east.

They had left the sand dunes behind more than an hour earlier, and were now crossing an almost flat plain. Winds had scoured most of the sand away, and they were marching across yellow earth, baked hard by the heat. Only in the hollows was there any sand, and Youba had to watch every patch of it for the footprints of the caravan. On the hard yellow earth it was impossible to see tracks of any kind.

Two minutes after the first gust of wind, a second came and swirled sand about. This gust lasted longer than the other. Omar El Hassim groaned. Youba shot a quick glance at his sister, but said nothing.

It was Fedada who said what the other two were thinking, "My brother, had we not better unload the camels and make ready? There will be more wind, and maybe a real sandstorm."

"Perhaps we could hurry, and get ahead of the wind," Omar suggested. "Men who cross the desert regularly tell me that the sandstorms are sometimes only a few miles wide."

His suggestion brought a mirthless laugh from Youba, who asked, "Can we fly like the vultures, sir? Can we make Tamerouelt walk quicker? She is a brave one to walk at all. Little Amr'r, too, limps as badly as his mother. And my sister is very tired — though she pretends not to be. We cannot hurry, so we must stop and unload. This place will do as well as any other. See, the wind is coming even now."

He pointed to what looked like a wall of smoke in the distance.

TEN

Sandstorm

Calling the camels to kneel, they unloaded the salt and built the six slabs into a wall. Together they helped Omar El Hassim behind the shelter the slabs made. While Fedada was scooping a comfortable place for herself behind the old man, Youba haltered the two camels. He did not halter Amr'r. The young camel would not leave his mother, of that he was sure.

By the time Youba had finished, the wind was blowing in savage gusts, driving before it a fog of gritty sand. No man could have stood for long in that wind-blasted yellow fog. It was impossible to see more than a dozen yards, and the sand would have peeled the skin from a man's face in minutes.

The camels were kneeling, their long necks outstretched, their nostrils closed to the merest slits so that they could take in air, but not sand. Youba hurriedly threw himself down by his sister, drew his cloak over his head, and prepared to endure the agonies of heat and thirst which lay ahead for all of them.

Howling like a demon, the wind blew at hurricane speed for minutes on end, then would die down to no more than a whisper. In those quiet moments it seemed as if it had lost its strength, but then, with a scream, it would come again, sand-laden and hot. The sand got everywhere. Despite the cloaks with which they covered their faces, Omar, Fedada, and Youba had sand on their eyelids, their lips, even in their nostrils.

The wind built sand up against the protecting salt slabs, then spilled over the top. It covered all of them with a layer several inches thick, increasing their discomfort, for it was like a covering of blankets, making them hotter and hotter.

Fedada soon drifted off into an uneasy sleep, but Youba could not sleep. A nagging doubt about the decision to bring Omar El Hassim along kept bothering him. The old man had helped them with Amr'r, but should he have risked his sister's life and his own for Omar? If he had not agreed to carry the salt, as well as its owner, they might have covered much more distance — might even have escaped the path of the sandstorm. If they had, they could have continued walking through the night and might have caught up with the caravan. Youba

was sick with worry. He seemed to have done so many wrong things.

Of one thing he was certain: they were very short of water, and after a sandstorm the wells were sometimes covered over. Then, only a man who had spent his life crossing and recrossing the desert could hope to find water.

Despite his fears Youba could not keep awake after an hour or so. The wind did not sound so wild now that they were covered by a layer of sand, and he fell into a doze. When he awoke a few hours later

his heart was beating fast, and he had a feeling
there was some terrible danger near.

Taut-nerved, and with every muscle tense in case
he had to leap up and run for his life, he lay and
listened. Only after a few minutes did he realize
that he had wakened in terror because of the silence.
The wind had dropped. Under the drifted sand he
could not hear even a whisper.

Shaking himself clear of the sand, he blinked at
the blue sky above him. The night had gone and the
day was at least an hour old. The desert was as

quiet as it usually was, with not a breath of wind moving. Wiping sand from his eyelashes Youba looked south.

When he had looked in that direction just before the sandstorm began, the way ahead had been flat, yellow earth, with here and there patches of soft sand, broken by the footprints of men and camels — showing the way the caravan had gone.

It was different now. The hard-baked, yellowish earth was covered by millions of tiny ripples of sand. They stretched ahead like the waves of an ocean, and there was not a footprint of any kind to be seen. The tracks they had been following, their guide to the next water hole, had all disappeared. The sand had filled them in, then covered them over. The trail had vanished.

Slowly Youba turned and scraped away the sand which covered Fedada. She woke and sat up, brushing yellow dust from her face, then pushing back her head covering so that she could shake some of the fine sand from her hair.

"What do we do now, my brother?" she asked, rising, then kneeling again to scrape the covering of sand from Omar El Hassim. "Shall we drink tea before we move on?"

Youba stared south for a few moments before replying, then he said quietly, "We can drink tea, my sister, but where we shall move to from here I do not know. Look at the way we have to go. There is no track of any kind. The sand has covered everything."

Fedada looked, and there was a quiver in her voice when she said bravely, "I will light a fire while you waken the old man. He will know. He is old, and years bring wisdom."

"I can waken him," Youba agreed, "and he will be glad of tea; but I do not think he can help us. If you remember, he said he had not been over this desert since he was a boy. How can he know where the wells are? He will be like a blind beggar, leading other blind beggars."

Fedada bent over and looked at the old man. His eyelids were fluttering a little, and she waited for him to waken. Then, to her surprise, one eye opened a fraction, but closed again.

Fedada moved back a few paces, but never took her eyes off the old man. She had a sudden feeling that he was awake, but was pretending to be asleep. Why he should do this she could not imagine; but after a few moments she thought she had guessed the answer. He must be trying to give her and Youba a chance to drink their tea and then leave him.

Turning to her brother, she said, "Youba, waken him. We must not stay here any longer than necessary. We should march before the heat becomes greater than we can bear."

Youba slipped to his knees beside the old man and began shaking him, first gently, then more vigorously. Fedada watched Omar El Hassim's face all the time. She saw his lips tighten, and she was sure then that he was only pretending to be asleep.

Youba, however, could get no response at all from the old man. Finally the boy rose, saying sadly, "I think he is dying, Fedada. Perhaps we should save his two glasses of tea. Later we shall need every drop of liquid that we can get. And while he lies there that way, he cannot drink."

"No, he is not dying, my brother," Fedada said urgently. "He is just pretending, so that we will use the water and leave him to die. Lift him up. Once the tea is at his lips he will drink. I know he will."

ELEVEN

The Camels Lead the Way

A few moments later Omar El Hassim was lifted into a sitting position. His eyes remained closed, though Youba could feel the muscles of the old man's upper arms tense, proving that he was not asleep.

Fedada put the glass of hot sweet tea to his mouth. The old man drew back as if it were poison, but Fedada moved the glass to his mouth again, and tilted it so that the tea was wetting his lips.

She had guessed right. That first taste of tea was an irresistible temptation to Omar. Lifting a hand, he steadied the glass and gulped the hot liquid.

His eyes opened and he looked at Youba and Fedada. He did not swallow the tea, but held it in his mouth, relishing the sweetness, and the wetness on his parched tongue. It was a beautiful sensation, but he had to swallow, and a moment later the tea was gone.

"There is more," Youba urged, nodding to his

sister to put the glass to the old man's lips again. "It will give you strength."

Omar shook his head sadly.

"Old men do not need to drink tea as younger ones do. Already I feel better. I have been thinking ..." He stopped talking when Fedada pressed the glass to his lips again. Giving her a smile, he finished what was left of the tea. "That was good, but I must drink no more. I have something important to say."

"There is another glass of tea for you," Fedada urged, but Omar shook his head, and waved a hand to keep her from picking up the little kettle.

"Listen to me, both of you. I know we are lost and that there is very little water. I know, too, that a limping camel walks too slowly. Take my camel and come back for me when you have found water."

Youba gave Fedada a long, questioning look, but she shook her head "No."

Rising, Youba went and got Tamerouelt and ordered the she-camel to kneel. Then, with Fedada helping him, the boy lifted the old man onto the camel's back.

Fedada gave Omar six dates, and apologized because she could not give him more. "We shall eat again the next time we stop," she promised.

Omar put a date into his mouth and began to

chew. Now that he was back in the saddle, he wanted to live. The glass of tea had given him a little strength, and more courage. To Youba he said, "This camel of mine I bought from a man who had walked it from Timbuktu to Taoudenni for seven years. Twice each year he carried salt on the beast. It must know the way to the water holes. Let it lead."

Fedada's eyes brightened, but clouded again when Youba reminded the old man: "You are forgetting, sir, that a camel goes forward only when he has a rider, or when a man pulls on his lead rope. I can lead the camel toward the midday sun, for I know Timbuktu lies that way. Whether I can find the next well, only Allah knows."

Omar nodded in agreement, but despite his exhaustion and the pain of his wound, he managed a little smile as he said, "When a camel needs water, my son, neither a rider nor a lead rope is necessary. If he is really thirsty, and if he knows where the water hole lies — he will walk."

Through the blistering heat they marched, halting at midday while Amr'r drank of his mother's milk, and Youba spread the prayer rug so that Omar El Hassim could kneel, and facing east toward Mecca, say his noonday prayers. The two children prayed with him.

While Fedada lit a small fire and made some tea, using water from the gerba her brother had found, Omar insisted on first massaging Amr'r's legs, then examining the injured foot.

After the fiercest heat of the day they continued south, and the sun seemed to dry up every drop of moisture from their bodies. They tried to eat a few dates, but swallowing was difficult.

Twice during that time Youba almost shrieked with joy at the sight of what he thought was a lake with palm trees ahead. But each time he realized within seconds that it was only a mirage — and it faded very quickly.

Then, toward the end of the afternoon, he swung around at a call for help from his sister. He was just in time to help Fedada prevent Omar El Hassim from falling heavily from the saddle. Gently they eased the old man to the ground. His eyes were closed, and he had apparently fainted.

They moistened his lips with a few drops of their precious water, and after a minute or so he recovered sufficiently to open his eyes, look up at them and whisper apologetically, "It is the leg wound. You will have to leave me. Each time my leg strikes against the camel's side it hurts abominably. You must go on and come back after you have found water."

"We cannot leave you, sir," Youba protested. "We may not find water until tomorrow. Then, how would we find you? If we stay here for a little while —"

"No, you must go now," Omar insisted. "As for finding me, if you leave some firewood I will light a little fire when darkness comes. The desert is very flat here and a fire will be seen for miles. Take my camel, but leave the salt. The camel will walk better with you than with me, for I am heavier than you."

"Sir, we cannot go on without you," Fedada exclaimed, and Youba added his reason why they could not do as the old man suggested:

"If we leave you, and you light a fire, it might be seen by the raiders."

Omar shook his head. "If the raiders came they would find nothing worth stealing. I have no jewels. You must go. I am an old man, old enough to be your grandfather. Were you not taught that it is not polite to disobey the wishes of an old man?"

"We were taught that, sir," Fedada agreed, "but it would not be right to leave you. If you were our grandfather — would we leave you?"

"How happy I would be if I had grandchildren like you," Omar said sadly. Then, brightening, he went on: "I was wrong when I insisted that we should bring along my salt. It has delayed us. But now I am going to insist that you go. Remember what I told you? The words of the Marabout, that 'Allah helps those who help themselves.' It is very true. You must . . . Aih! See, the camels are on their way to water. Even they know that time is too precious to waste. Follow them, or it will be too late."

Fedada and Youba turned in sudden panic at the old man's words, and Youba scrambled to his feet. Omar was right. His big, scrawny-looking camel was striding south, and because Tamerouelt's lead

rope was secured to him, she had to follow. Little
Amr'r was trotting obediently behind his mother.
The three camels were already some distance away.

Yelling for them to halt, Youba began to run;
but he was tired, and the camels had been walking
for several minutes. After a minute the boy had to
stop. He was weaker than he had imagined, and
the camels were walking briskly, even the lame
Tamerouelt and the slightly limping Amr'r.

Returning to where Fedada was kneeling by
Omar, Youba agreed they would have to leave him.
They gave him matches and some sticks, then
turned without a word to follow their camels.

For three miles they struggled to catch up, but
hardly gained a yard. Then the camels began to
increase their lead as Fedada's leg weariness increased. Finally brother and sister were forced to
rely on the camel tracks. Tired and despairing, they
walked on until they came to the beginning of a
gorge. Its rocky sides were already beginning to
cast long shadows, for the sun was dropping toward the western horizon. In less than an hour
night would be on them.

Youba and Fedada paused at the entrance to the
gorge, looking down. It was as if some long-dead
giant had scooped a deep channel from the desert
itself. The rocky walls were pink, and at the top

where the rays of the setting sun lit them, they glowed as if on fire. The entrance was like the neck of a bottle, but inside the gorge widened quickly. Boulders littered its floor, and there was a strange eeriness about the place.

Fedada clutched at her brother's sleeve, but Youba pointed to camel tracks between the boulders. Shoving their fears aside, the two of them walked into the gorge. They could feel cool air moving soundlessly past them, here where the sun could not reach. Then, farther down where the gorge reached its greatest width, they saw the three camels and at once their anxieties were forgotten.

Tamerouelt and the other camel were kneeling by a rocky pool, their long necks outstretched, while little Amr'r stood patiently by his mother's side. He knew that when she had drunk her fill, there would be rich milk for him.

"They are drinking," Fedada whispered. "My brother, they have found water."

Youba could have run, but Fedada was too tired, so they both walked slowly on. The camels had done it, Youba thought. They had found water. As soon as he and his sister had satisfied their own thirsts and refilled the almost empty gerba, they could go back for Omar El Hassim. Neither he nor Fedada spoke, for they were too filled with joy. At the moment, it seemed as if all their worries were over.

Only when they were about thirty yards from the three camels did they hear a sound. Looking to the left they stopped, and caught their breath. More than a dozen camels were squatting by the rocky wall of the gorge, half hidden by a clutter of boulders. From behind the boulders came half a dozen men, all of them armed. They were dark-featured and travel-stained; one had a bandaged arm.

Youba and Fedada guessed at once that they were members of the raiding party.

TWELVE

Held for Ransom

Fedada sank to her knees, and Youba stepped protectively in front of her. At this one of the men shouted an order to another who hurried over with a full gerba of water. Surrounded by the fierce-looking band, Youba waited, wondering what was going to happen. Then the gerba was shoved neck first toward him.

Indicating that his sister needed the water more, Youba stepped aside. The man sprayed water over Fedada's face to revive her, then gave her a drink. When she had taken all she wanted, it was Youba's turn. He drank until perspiration began to cover his face, neck, and arms.

Only then, when both children had drunk their fill, did the hawk-faced man who seemed to be the leader of the party ask: "Where is the rest of the caravan?"

"We were left behind, sir," Youba said, shrugging. "We were trying to rejoin the caravan, but could move only slowly. The she-camel was struck by a bullet, and the old man was also wounded."

"Old man," the leader of the party said suspiciously. "What old man?"

"We had to leave him," Youba explained. Bending down, he helped his sister to her feet and led her toward the pool where their camels were still drinking. The group of men followed, conversing among themselves in short, rapid sentences. Then, after Youba had made Fedada as comfortable as he could on a smooth slab of rock, with a big stone to lean against, the leader asked, "Who is this old man? Is he a merchant? What has he got with him?"

"He has nothing." Youba tried to keep his voice calm, but nervousness made it quiver. Pointing to the big camel carrying Omar's six slabs of salt, he added, "That is all he has. He is just an old man returning to Timbuktu where he hopes to spend his days in peace. I promised to take water to him."

"Water!" one of the men sneered. "If he had merchandise we would see he got water. But if he has nothing — let him end his days in the desert. We have no time for penniless merchants."

"You would not let a harmless old man die, sir!" Youba cried in astonishment. "I promised that if I found water I would return and bring him to safety. Won't you let me do that? He has been very kind to me and my sister. Please let me return to him."

After a long discussion, interrupted by angry shouts from some members of the band, the leader turned to tell Youba that he would be allowed to go back for Omar. He could take Tamerouelt and the old man's camel. The young Amr'r and Fedada would remain with the band in the gorge.

While the salt was being unloaded from Omar's camel, one of the raiders saddled his own animal. He had been ordered to accompany Youba.

Before mounting Tamerouelt, Youba spoke with his sister. There, at the gorge bottom, almost all daylight had gone and he had trouble seeing Fedada's face. But he could feel her hands trembling as he took them in his own.

"No harm will come to you, my sister," he insisted. "They do not know where the old man is, and since one of them is coming with me, they will not leave here before I return."

Fedada merely nodded, but her grip on Youba's hands tightened as he turned to go to Tamerouelt. She was even more frightened a few moments later when she heard the leader of the band say to Youba, "Don't try to lead the way into a trap. Remember, your sister is here with us, and if anything goes wrong, she will die."

Fedada shivered and closed her eyes. She heard

the creak of leather as her brother settled into the saddle and she almost called to him not to leave her — but she stopped herself at the last moment. Old Omar was depending on Youba.

Youba, too, went cold with fear at the leader's warning. He bent his head and whispered: "Allah, help us. There is no one else who can."

Then the raider who was to go with him swung into the saddle. Tamerouelt lurched to her feet at a snarled command, and they were on their way. Little Amr'r, who had been tethered to a rock, tried to follow Tamerouelt, and for the first time Youba heard his own young camel bawling angrily at being parted from his mother.

For half an hour Youba and the Moor rode north, the moon showing on the horizon as a lightening of the starry sky. When it finally lifted above the horizon its cold white light seemed to make the stars grow paler.

Youba was growing anxious. Even with the moon it was impossible to see tracks in the sand. They did not seem to be returning the way they had come. In the uncertain moonlight a man needed to be no more than a few yards off a trail to miss seeing the telltale tracks of camels.

"What is that?" The man riding with Youba pulled his camel to a stop and pointed.

"Ah, Allah be praised," Youba whispered. "I left the old man with firewood, and he was to light a fire to guide me back."

As they drew nearer and the red spot was showing larger, the man with Youba said threateningly, "Remember, if you are leading me into a trap, the girl will die."

"There is no trap, sir," Youba insisted. "Only a tired old man."

In ten minutes he proved he was telling the truth. Omar El Hassim was sitting by the little fire, his head bowed. He was on the point of collapse, but he revived when water from the full gerba they had brought along was splashed into his face. Then, like

Youba, and Fedada, and the camels, he drank as if he were made of blotting paper.

A little over an hour later they were back in the deep-sided gorge. Cooking fires were burning, and the raiders gave Youba, Fedada, and Omar a meal of meat and rice. The raiders had shot a desert gazelle earlier in the day, and the smell of cooking meat was something Youba and Fedada had not known for a long time. Youba noticed that Fedada ate almost nothing, but then she had been through so much that day. Old Omar was utterly exhausted and sank into a doze before the meal was even over.

The raiders posted a guard at each end of the gorge, and then with the fires out, lay down to sleep. Youba and his sister lay within touching distance, and when everything was quiet, Fedada reached out a hand to her brother, and whispered, "I am frightened. The men have been talking while you were away."

"Talking about us?"

Fedada nodded.

"What did they say?"

"They thought I was asleep," Fedada whimpered, "and they were arguing about what to do with me. Youba, they may take me to the Spanish Sahara with them and sell me."

"Sell you!" Youba was horror-stricken. "As a slave?"

"That is what some of them wanted," Fedada said, stifling a sob. "I think they finally decided to send you to the oasis at Araouane first."

"If they do that, then I could get help —"

"No, no — you couldn't," Fedada interrupted. "These men need camels. Most of their own animals were injured when they attacked our uncle's caravan a second time — that is why they were left behind by the other raiders. You are to go to Araouane and bring back twenty camels for them. A ransom they called it. Twenty of the best riding camels. If you don't come back . . . then I will be taken away to be sold."

"Twenty riding camels," Youba whispered. "But who would give us twenty such beasts? Even our father possesses only forty, and he has worked hard all his life to acquire them. No one would give me twenty camels. Oh, Fedada, my little sister!"

He drew her to him and cradled her head against his shoulder. At length Fedada cried herself to sleep, and Youba eased her gently to the ground and just as gently drew her hood up over her head to protect her against the night cold.

He did not try to sleep. Instead he lay and stared

at the sky, trying to think of some way to save his sister. Collecting twenty riding camels to buy her freedom seemed as hopeless as trying to reach a hand up to the moon.

His father and the first caravan would be many miles beyond Araouane by now, for they had started south a week before the smaller caravan. Whether the second caravan had reached the oasis, Youba had no idea. But even they would be more than a day's journey ahead of him. They had probably not been caught in the sandstorm, and they would not be traveling slowly. Their speed would be much greater than had been the speed of Tamerouelt and little Amr'r.

The more he tried to think of something, the more hopeless it seemed. When the moon rose above the top of the gorge and bathed everything in its clean, cold white light, he raised himself on one elbow and looked carefully around.

He was wondering if there might be a chance of escape. The raiders all seemed to be sleeping soundly. The camels were asleep in a circle, heads pointing to the center. He wondered if it might be possible for him and Fedada to take a camel each near dawn, when the moon was no longer shining down the gorge. That last hour before the new day was

always the darkest. It was the right time for anyone with courage to make a dash for freedom.

Then he remembered Omar. The old man could
not hope to ride a fast-moving camel, and Youba
knew what would happen to him if the raiders lost
their chance of a ransom. Omar El Hassim would
die. No one would pay a ransom for him! Youba
sighed and lay down again; how could he save his
sister?

THIRTEEN

Omar Takes Charge

Dawn came with the air still bitterly cold. The raiders cooked a meal, using what was left of the gazelle. Then Youba was taken before the leader of the band, who wasted no words when he explained to the boy what was going to happen.

"No man rides a thousand miles for nothing," the leader said harshly. "And one girl is a better prize than returning home empty-handed. You will ride to the next oasis, which is Araouane. Gather twenty of the best riding camels and bring them back to me. If you do that, your sister will be handed over unharmed. I shall wait five days, no more. If you have not returned at the end of that time, you will never see the girl again."

So Fedada had been right.

"I will give you my young camel," Youba pleaded. "He comes of the finest mehari blood. One day he will be a champion. He will win desert races . . ."
There he stopped, for the leader and several of the

raiders were laughing contemptuously at him. But the laughter ended as suddenly as it began when the leader said sharply:

"Twenty riding camels — and good ones, or the girl comes with us."

Youba looked across at Fedada who was sitting a few yards away, her head bowed. He caught sight of Omar El Hassim, and asked hesitantly, "And what of the old man. Does he stay?"

"He can go with you," was the leader's impatient reply. "We cannot feed a beggar, and he is of no use to us."

They were given two gerbas of water, some pounded millet and goat cheese, and fodder for the two camels. When Youba pleaded that he be allowed to take Amr'r with him, he was cuffed savagely across the side of the head.

"No. We may need meat before you return. He could provide us with food."

Youba winced at the thought. He was about to make a last plea for Amr'r when Omar El Hassim hobbled over to ask if he might take two slabs of salt with him to Araouane.

"It would fetch money," the old man said quickly, before the raider leader could yell at him. "At least it would go toward the cost of one of the twenty camels."

"Take what salt you wish," was the man's angry retort, "but you cannot have another camel to carry it. And don't ask for anything else, or you'll get a bullet instead."

"We can't afford to carry any salt," Youba whispered to Omar as they went to saddle the camels. "We must hurry as we have never hurried before."

"But one slab of salt on each camel will make so little difference," Omar urged. "And if I sell the salt, who knows, we may be able to pay something toward a camel."

"Will two blocks of salt buy a camel?" Youba asked bitterly, yet there was so much anxiety in the old man's eyes that finally he nodded agreement.

While Youba prepared the camels, loading a slab of salt on each, Fedada washed and rebandaged Omar El Hassim's bullet wound. The germ-free air of the desert was helping it to heal, but the old man would limp for some weeks.

Amr'r was given a feed by his mother. It was the last he would have from her for some days, and Fedada promised Youba to sort some of the best fodder for him. Amr'r had already begun to eat a little camel food, so at least he would not starve while Tamerouelt was away.

Youba and Fedada helped Omar El Hassim onto

his camel, and Youba was about to climb onto Tam-erouelt's back when his sister spoke.

"Allah be with you, my brother," Fedada said, trying hard to keep her voice steady. "Travel quickly. I shall look for you on the fifth day."

"Maybe it will be the fourth day," Youba said, but deep down he was afraid that he might never see her again. Usually the people of an oasis were poor. They had a few date palms; they kept goats and a few sheep. Some owned camels, but they hired them to caravan men whose own beasts came in overworked, or limping. There would be riding camels, but who would let a boy have twenty of the beasts in the hope that his father would be able to pay for them later on?

The leader of the party rode with Omar and Youba to the south end of the gorge. There he gave them instructions on how to reach Araouane. The way was due south, and not difficult, for the oasis lay on the far side of a ridge of hills. In the middle of the ridge there was a gash which led directly to Araouane.

"Remember, I give you five days," the leader warned. Then he wheeled his camel around and turned back into the gorge.

Throughout the first day hardly a word passed

between Youba and the old man. Omar El Hassim was still shaky from his wound, and his experience in the desert. They slept the first night under the desert moon, with their camels leg-haltered nearby. Neither had traveled over this route without a guide. Yet there were tracks now, for they were in a region where the caravan had passed after the sandstorm.

Toward the end of the second day, they were still pushing their camels as hard as they could. Tamerouelt's limp had almost gone, and she was now striding out like the thoroughbred she was.

Ahead of them, on the skyline, Youba could make out a ridge, and in the middle of it a V-shaped nick. "That must be the gash," he said. "And just beyond is Araouane."

"It is a long way," Omar said soberly. "I don't know if I can ride there without a rest."

"I, too, am tired," Youba said, "but *I* am riding. When the sun sets, two of the five days will be gone. It will take at least two days to get back to the gorge, and Fedada. Rest if you will. I will leave you all the water and food so that you —"

"No, I will come with you," Omar said, though his face was lined with weariness. "The sun is setting. Let us stop and pray."

They dismounted, and while Youba held the camels, Omar got out his little praying mat, spread it on the sands, and bowed five times in the direction of Mecca as he said his evening prayers.

It was well past midnight when they slithered down the pass into Araouane. The palm trees looked silvery in the light of the moon, and so did the tops of the mud-brick houses, but neither Youba nor Omar had eyes for beauty. The old man was reeling in the saddle from weariness. Youba was tired and saddle-sore, but no matter how exhausted he was he knew he had to find the sheikh who ruled the oasis.

"Rest by the well," Youba suggested, helping Omar to climb out of the saddle. "When I have seen the sheikh, then I will come and prepare food for you."

"A son could not say more than that," Omar said, "so I am going to try to behave to you as a father would. *I* will come to speak with the sheikh for you."

They walked slowly, their weary camels following at their heels. There were lights showing in many of the houses. When the sun shines like a ball of molten fire during the day, those who have to live in its heat year in and year out learn to rest in the shade at midday, and often work through half the night.

At one of the houses Youba stopped to ask where the sheikh lived and was told to follow the street to its end.

The sheikh's house was in darkness, and to Youba's surprise, Omar El Hassim asked him to take his camel's headrope, saying, "I will see what the sheikh can do for you. Sometimes an older man commands respect, even if only because of his gray hairs."

Youba sat cross-legged by the wall of the house, half dozing, while the two camels sank to their knees, glad of a chance to rest their long thin legs.

Ten minutes passed and Youba was almost asleep when a servant hurried out of the house and, after a quick look at the camels, began to take off one of the slabs of salt. Youba woke and stopped the

man, but just then Omar came out, and with him the sheikh.

"I asked that a servant be called to unload the salt," Omar explained.

Puzzled and still half-asleep, Youba followed the old man through the courtyard into the house, where they were shown into the main room. The only furniture was a long, very low table and a number of leather cushions. The windows were glassless, but protected by ornamental iron bars. Moonlight streamed in through one window, brilliant enough to show even when an oil lamp was brought in and placed on the earthen floor.

The sheikh was a tall, imposing man with fierce eyes. His thin nostrils seemed to quiver as he stared distastefully at the travel-stained Youba and Omar.

The servant came in with a huge pitcher of water, but before he could set it on the floor, Omar ordered him to pour the water over one of the slabs of salt.

The servant's eyes widened in astonishment, and he turned to look at his master as if half expecting the sheikh to tell him not to obey the order. Youba gasped. To pour water on salt was like throwing money away.

There was a strange little smile on Omar's face as he pointed to the salt and repeated his command. The old man looked tired and dirty, yet he spoke like one who was accustomed to giving orders, and having them obeyed.

"You want water poured on your salt?" the sheikh asked incredulously. "You told me you had something wonderful to show me. This is not wonderful — it is madness. Are you so wealthy that you can waste good salt? I will buy it from you."

"O Sheikh," Omar said calmly, "the wise man waits to see if what he thinks is foolish really is foolish. Does an old man throw wealth away? The young may be foolish, but old men are different. Tell your servant to pour as I command."

FOURTEEN

The Secret
of the Salt Blocks

Still round-eyed with wonder, the servant poured
water onto the slab of salt. For perhaps a minute
nothing happened. Some of the water soaked into
the slab, while more poured off it onto the earthen
floor. Then came little creaks and crackles from inside the salt as the fifty-pound block began to ex-
pand and break.

The only other sounds came from the watchers.
All were breathing hard. Youba stood tense and
expectant, sure that something miraculous was
about to happen. As more water was poured over
the block, the salt changed into a slushy mass.

Omar asked the sheikh to send the gaping servant
from the room, and took the pitcher himself. Then
he began to slowly spread out the heap of water-
softened salt. Youba and the sheikh stared intently
at his busy hands.

It was the sheikh who broke the silence with a gasp when Omar uncovered a salt-encrusted leather bag. The old man laid it by his side and went on probing the salt, taking out one bag after another until six sat next to each other on the floor, the wet leather glistening in the yellow lamplight.

"What is inside?" the sheikh asked. He had been

haughty a few minutes earlier, but now his stiff manner had changed. He was suddenly very friend-ly, showing his long teeth in an ingratiating smile.

Omar did not answer him, but turning to Youba said quietly, "Back in the desert I told you that if I lost my six blocks of salt I would be a penniless beggar. What I did not tell you was that after forty years of hard work in Taoudenni, first as a laborer, and finally as a salt merchant, I sold all I had —"

"And this is money?" Youba's eyes were gleam-ing now. "We would be able . . . " He was going to say they would be able to buy camels, but Omar in-terrupted him.

Turning to the sheikh, he said, "In Taoudenni men knew the salt merchant Abd Osman E'uk. You have heard the name?"

"I *have* heard the name," the sheikh agreed. "Did he not own one of the best salt pits? Was he not said to be a rich man?"

Youba looked at Omar El Hassim, his mouth agape. Suddenly he knew the truth. Omar El Has-sim must be Abd Osman E'uk. And if he really were that man, then buying twenty riding camels would not be impossible.

"Two months ago I caused a story to be spread around that I had gone away on business," Omar said, a little smile crinkling the corners of his mouth. "I did not want anyone to know that I planned to travel back to Timbuktu with my savings. Abd Osman E'uk was a clean-shaven man. When a man who called himself Omar El Hassim appeared in Taoudenni, gray-haired, gray-bearded, and dressed in the poorest clothes, no one guessed he was the wealthy Abd Osman E'uk."

The sheikh clapped his hands, and when the servant appeared, he called immediately for coffee, and for clean clothes for his guests. While he was doing this, Omar was untying the neck of one of the leather bags.

Youba watched in wonder as the old man tipped a little pile of gold coins out onto the floor. He could scarcely breathe for excitement. Omar spread the coins out and counted them into little piles. There was a warm chuckle in his voice when he said, "Youba, who befriended me when I most needed a friend, your sister shall not die for the want of twenty camels."

And to the sheikh: "My friend, as you see I am not the penniless old beggar you first thought me when your servant called you. I promised to show you a wonderful thing. Now I will do more. Send your servants to buy twenty of the best riding camels . . . and there shall be a gift for you that you will remember for a long time."

In minutes the quiet house was all astir. Servants were summoned to prepare a meal. Others were sent to tell camel men that when dawn came they were to bring their best meharis to the sheikh's home.

After they had eaten, Omar was taken to the best room. Youba was led to a smaller room containing a long leather couch. There a servant massaged him as Omar El Hassim had once massaged little Amr'r, soothing the aches from his tired body. The man used oils which made the rubdown even more pleasant. When he finally put stoppers on his bottles and bowed to Youba, there was not an ache or a pain left in the boy's body.

Shown to another room, Youba lay down, and fell asleep almost at once. An hour after sunrise he was awakened and offered coffee and food. Then Omar El Hassim came in to ask him to come out and choose camels.

In the full glare of the morning sun more than fifty riding camels were gathered, their owners beginning to shout to Omar El Hassim about the strength, speed, and beauty of their animals — and their cheapness.

Omar was dressed in a spotless white robe, and wearing a magnificent headdress he looked a very

different person indeed from the Omar El Hassim who had pretended he was no more than a poor old man traveling to Timbuktu to end his days.

Soon after midday twenty splendid riding camels had been chosen, and paid for. With them went two work camels, who would carry Fedada and the four slabs of salt Omar had been forced to leave behind in the gorge where the raiders were waiting for the ransom.

The sheikh, who could not be friendly enough to Omar El Hassim now that he knew what a rich man he was, suggested that he would provide a party of armed men to go with the camels.

"No," Omar said firmly. "If one armed man goes along, the raiders will kill the girl and then vanish into the desert." He turned to Youba, "If she were my own grandchild I would not take greater care of your sister Fedada. But I am too old and tired to ride back with the camels. You will do that."

The old man clasped Youba's shoulder, then shifted his gaze back to the sheikh. "He is only a boy, but he has the strength of youth. Send one good camel man along with him. That will be enough."

That was how they went, Youba riding an impatient Tamerouelt who seemed to realize they were heading back to the place where she had been parted from her son, Amr'r.

Two hours before sunset on the fifth day, Youba led the long string of riding camels into the mouth of the gorge, still sunlit, and apparently deserted. The camel man who had ridden with him had stayed some miles behind with the two camels who would carry the salt and Fedada back to Araouane. Neither Youba nor the camel man wanted to risk having the raiders take those camels in addition to the twenty.

Half way into the gorge, Youba was surrounded by the raiders. A scout had alerted them that the camels were approaching, and had made sure there was no armed party with them. Youba was about to dismount to speak to the band's leader when Tamerouelt suddenly gave a bleating bellow. Out went her long neck, and do what he could, Youba could not halt her.

Like a true racing camel she sped smoothly and swiftly down to the spot where little Amr'r, looking leaner after five days without his mother's milk, was tethered to a rock. Nearby stood a smiling Fedada. Youba was almost thrown over the mother camel's neck as she slid to a stop and began nosing her son, who immediately ducked his head and began to feed.

Fedada helped Youba down from the saddle. She had been told that the camel train was coming, and

now Youba was actually here. Both of them were too overwhelmed to speak, but their eyes expressed their happiness at being together again.

By this time the raiders had checked on the twenty camels, and the leader came up, a half smile on his hawklike face.

"And what would you say now if I took the twenty camels, *and* your sister?" he asked.

Youba swung around, the joy wiped off his face in a flash. But before he could say anything in reply the Moor laughed and shook his head. "Don't be

afraid. I am a man of my word, boy. You have kept
your part of the agreement. I keep mine. At dawn
we go. Come, we have prepared food."

Youba walked with Fedada to the sheltered spot
where several cooking fires were burning, and food
was set out in bowls in front of groups of five.
Youba and Fedada sat with three of the raiders.
The leader asked about Araouane, and smiled when
Youba said he had seen little of the oasis.

"I am not seeking information so that we can
raid the place," he chuckled. "We are heading north

to lick our wounds. This has been a bad year for us."

That night, with guards again set at each end of the gorge, they all lay down to sleep. Little Amr'r, whose injured foot was now almost completely healed, had settled as close to his mother as possible. He did not want to be separated from her again.

In the silence, broken only by the sound of water falling drop by drop out of the rocks into the tiny pool, Fedada and Youba were able to talk alone for the first time since his return.

"My heart is heavy for our father," Fedada said. "He will lose half his camels to pay for those twenty riding camels . . . and all because of me."

Youba patted his sister gently on the shoulder, and there was happiness in his voice when he said, "My sister, let your heart grow light. You now have a *grandfather:* Omar El Hassim . . . though his real name is Abd Osman E'uk. He is not a poor old man. He is rich, very rich, and —"

"Abd Osman E'uk?" Fedada was confused.

"He changed his name, and grew a beard, so that he could travel in the caravan without anyone knowing he was a wealthy man." And Youba went on to tell his sister about the amazing blocks of salt.

Fedada sat up and looked toward the rocky wall of the gorge where the four remaining blocks of

Omar's salt shone like snow in the light of the moon. "Allah must have guided us, my brother, when we agreed to take the salt with us. How near we were to leaving it behind!"

"Yes." Youba frowned as he remembered how he had shouted at Omar, and had almost insisted that the salt be abandoned in the desert.

"Allah is great," Fedada whispered, "to give us such a wonderful friend as Omar. Did he not save Amr'r, and then me? How can we ever repay him?"

Suddenly her expression became very serious. "My brother," she said, "we must look after Tamerouelt and Amr'r all our lives."

"Well, of course," Youba agreed, puzzled. "After all, Tamerouelt is one of our father's favorite camels . . . and Amr'r is my first camel. My very own camel. But why do you say we must especially look after them?"

"If Tamerouelt had not given birth to Amr'r, and if Amr'r had not been so weary, we would never have come to know Omar El Hassim. We might not have been awake the morning when the raiders attacked. We might all have been killed."

"I had not thought of that," Youba said, and nodded his understanding. "The ways of life are strange, and very wonderful. But now, my sister, we must sleep. It is a long ride to Araouane."

FIFTEEN

Home to Timbuktu

An hour after dawn the next morning, Youba and Fedada watched the band of raiders ride off. They left behind some of their own injured camels, whose bullet wounds prevented them from traveling as quickly as their owners desired.

While Fedada lit a fire and prepared food, Youba rode out of the gorge to the south and signaled to the camel man waiting with the other camels. He came up to drink tea and eat a meal before the return journey.

The raiders' camels were linked nose to tail, and the two-day walk to Araouane began. Omar's four precious blocks of salt were on a camel linked to the one Youba rode. Fedada rode Tamerouelt, at whose tail Amr'r walked. He was friskier now than he had been since birth. His injured foot was practically healed, and he was growing quickly in strength and endurance.

When they were still several miles from the oasis, men on camels came to meet them, and sight of the leading rider made the eyes of both Youba and Fedada light up in wonder and delight. It was their Uncle Abbah.

"A man on a fast mehari came after the caravan, sent by old Omar," Uncle Abbah explained. "Oh, the joy when I got the news that you both were alive! The messenger did not tell me that you were being held for ransom," he added, looking anxiously at Fedada. "Are you all right — the raiders didn't harm you?"

"No, no, I am fine," Fedada said, smiling.

"No one expected to see either of you alive again," Uncle Abbah continued. "In the confusion of the raid there was no time to think. When I started to hurry to the end of the camel lines to look for you, I got this." Pulling back his sleeve he showed them a bandage. "A bullet through the arm. But Allah be praised . . . you are safe, and now I can look my brother, your father, in the eyes and not be too ashamed."

The days which followed in Araouane were like a wonderful dream for Youba and Fedada. Omar El Hassim called them both to the sheikh's house, where he was staying, to see him break open the last four blocks of salt and uncover his wealth. The old man was as excited as a small boy.

Omar did not intend to wait for a caravan going

to Timbuktu. From Araouane there was little danger of being attacked by desert raiders, but even so Omar was taking no chances. He had hired eight armed men to guard them on the homeward journey.

"Your uncle and I have sent a man on a fast camel to Timbuktu to let your father know that you are safe," he announced, adding: "There is a saying that evil news travels on the wings of the morning. I hope our messenger will travel even faster."

It was a long trek through the desert to Timbuktu, and even when they could see the last ridge of tall sand dunes that separated them from their home, the distance seemed slow to lessen.

Then they saw a man on a camel.

"That will be your father," Uncle Abbah prophesied, and he was right. On his fastest camel, Moussa came hurrying out to meet the little caravan.

Fedada cried on her father's shoulder from sheer happiness when Moussa lifted her down from Tamerouelt and carried her in his arms to where Omar El Hassim sat astride his camel.

"My house is your house forever," Moussa said, setting Fedada down and reaching up to take the

old man's hands in his. "I have heard the whole story. Only the closest friend, or a brother, would have given twenty camels to save a child like my Fedada."

The brown eyes of Omar twinkled as he said, "My friend, I gave twenty camels, but your son and daughter gave me my life. Thus can I say in return to you: when I have bought a house, its doors will always be open to you and yours."

Greetings over, they marched on to Timbuktu, its houses glistening in the brilliant sunshine. Friends hailed them as they passed through the crowded bazaar, and then the camels walked sedately into the courtyard of Moussa's house.

Youba and Fedada lingered outside while the others went into the house. Youba bent down and affectionately tickled Amr'r's back leg, and grunted when the little camel gave him a swift kick on the shin.

"My brother, when will you learn?" Fedada said, laughing, as they walked toward the stable. "A high-born camel does not allow himself to be tickled like a baby."

They led Tamerouelt into the best stall, and brought her water and fodder. Amr'r began to feed. Soon he would no longer be taking his mother's milk, but for the moment, that was all he wanted.

"Are you going to look at his foot?" Fedada asked when they were about to leave and go into the house.

"My sister, I have just *felt* his foot," Youba said, "and I do not think there is anything wrong with it now. He kicks like a full-grown bull camel!"

Turning from his feeding, Amr'r gave a little snort, almost as though he were replying to Youba. The boy smiled. "Come, Fedada," he said, "we must help our father welcome Omar to our house."